#ShidduchCrisis

-Short Stories

Penina Shtauber

First printing 2019

ISBN 978-965-92757-0-0

This book is dedicated to Tzippy

#crisisaverted

Forty days before the child is formed, a Heavenly voice proclaims that the daughter of a designated person will be his wife.

Rabbi Yehuda, Sotah, 2a

shid·duch cri·sis

/'SHidəKH,SHi'do͞oKH/ /'krīsis/

noun

A commonly observed and discussed phenomenon in the Orthodox Jewish community whereby eligible single persons, especially women, have difficulty finding a suitable spouse, or a **shidduch.**

// *"Ma! I'll never get married. There's a **shidduch crisis**!"*

Author's Note

A friend of mine asked me why I don't write happy stories. I told her that she could ask her mom for a happy story. Or her neighbor, or her cousin, or her friends on Facebook. Who doesn't love sharing a nice, happy story? Happy stories are *everywhere*.

Happy stories are boring.

And happy is not the only version of reality that exists.

Reality is also sad, complicated, confusing and ironic. Real stories aren't censored. Some make you think. Some make you laugh. Some challenge your morals so much, they bother you inside.

Dating is a small step in life that determines a major outcome. There is a lot of happiness, but also a lot of everything else. I tried to encompass it all.

Contents

Her Short Skirt Said it All

It's not even my fault. I blame *her*. She asked for it.

Our first date and she wore a tight black skirt with a slit up the back. She thought I wouldn't notice... or worse, she hoped I would. The whole date I had my eyes over her shoulder, self-conscious that the whole lobby was watching, she spoke loudly and used wild hand gestures. When I told her the story about the fake mouse we planted in our Rebbe's drawer in middle school, she shrieked in laughter and I turned red.

Rachel was a one-date type of girl, the type I'd say no to, and she'd be fine with it... because she'd say no back.

The thing is, I didn't. Something about her, the way she smiled easily and uncalculated, was more genuine than any other girl I'd gone out with yet. And surprise, surprise, she said yes to going out with me too.

Our second date was more intimate, a nice café in Mamilla. We got food this time. I ordered a light salad and she shamelessly chose the salmon and a side of string beans. She beamed when it came and she beamed at me, her smile was worth coming out here for.

When the waiter cleared our plates, she suggested we get dessert. My father gave me a hundred shekel for the date and that barely covered her dinner alone but I nodded anyway.

"I'm fine," I said, "you get whatever you want."

She ordered the Belgian waffle with ice cream on top.

"Are you having a nice time?" She asked, "I know I'm not supposed to ask, but I'm curious." She leaned over and flashed one of her careless smiles.

My heart beat faster. I'd never been confronted like this before. She'd hear it from the *shadchan* tomorrow or the day after, why was she asking me now? It was also endearing, how straight up she was like I said: unashamed.

"Yeah, this is really," I cleared my throat, "... nice. Really nice."

Did this mean I'd have to go out with her again? Did I want to go out with her again? She looked at me with wide eyes and it was hard not to notice her beauty. Her smooth skin and thick... ahem... lips.

I averted my eyes so she wouldn't catch me staring, so I wouldn't catch myself staring.

She said yes, she wanted to go out with me again. Between the second and third date, I couldn't think of anything else but her. I closed my eyes during *Shmoneh Esrei* and her face popped up, clear as reality—thick hair, now I could appreciate how thick and shiny it was, her eyelids heavy and always sparkly. Her lips—

How did she do it? How did she keep her lips pink? When my mother drank Kiddush wine on Friday night her lipstick stained the cup. It was completely wiped out by the time we were done with the first course. Rachel's lasted the whole evening, imprinted itself on my memory. Her laugh—that irksome, exaggerated laugh—rang in my head. It even made me smile.

I said yes for the wrong reasons I realized. I said yes because I was attracted to her physical appearance. I said yes because I wanted to see her because I wanted... her.

Why did she say yes to me?

It was her fault more than anything but I'll also take some blame. The third date I borrowed my parent's car to pick her up. A bad idea, the worst idea. It wasn't acceptable and I knew why—the exact reason I chose to use it.

I picked her up and it was okay. We drove around and it was okay, still okay.

"Where do you want to go?" I asked.

"Whatever you want," she said.

So we drove in circles around the neighborhood because that was all I wanted—to be alone with her. A hundred voices went against me in my head, my parents—they were appalled, Rabbi Shalom—he shook his head in dismay, even Shlomo, my *chavruta* who I knew went off the *derech* when he was a teen even if he never spoke about it.

Mostly I heard Your voice. You looked down at me and said, "My boy, is this really want you want? You know I only give you tests you can overcome."

I caught Rachel's eyes, she grinned on automatic, teeth white and shining, lips that candy pink, and I knew, this test I could not overcome.

This is why I don't go out with modern girls, they wear their long hair down and their skirts so short they ride up when they sit. Did she realize it hit mid-thigh? Her knees glistened in sheer pantyhose.

Eventually, I parked the car in an underground lot near a shopping mall.

She moved to open her door but I leaned back in my seat, "we could stay here for a bit," I said, "If you'd like?"

"Sure," she said and leaned on her own seat, brushing her hair to one side.

This was what they spoke about when they said *'Yetzer Hara'*, this was the feeling: her perfume thick in the air, her eyelids so heavy they'd drop in a minute, drop her into a dream and with luck I'd be in that dream with her. Somehow her neckline dipped too, showed off her defined collar bones and even below. At first, I averted my eyes, but then I looked at the trail of skin and the shadows formed. And then I stared. Rachel smiled knowingly, she smiled the whole time.

She even smiled when she sat up and said, "Actually, I think we should go to the mall. It's gonna close soon."

I laughed and said no. I told her we should stay, I told her we'd go later, another time, you're having a nice time, aren't you Rachel?

She cleared her throat like I did and laughed, "of course."

Oh, why did You give me a test I was destined to fail? Why did You send Rachel my way?

It wasn't fair, it wasn't fair that her skin looked smoother than any skin I've seen, that her nails were filed and baby pink and perfect. That she was the manifestation of feelings I'd read about, feeling that I wasn't supposed to have, that I was supposed to keep for my wife. This woman wasn't my wife, wouldn't be my wife. She was nice to look at and surprising and refreshing, but she wouldn't make a good wife. Even though she shut her eyes and hummed a tune I didn't know and I felt fire and I didn't know what to do with it. She wouldn't be my wife so I didn't need that fire.

What could I have done?

I sinned.

Is there anything more to say?

Was it my fault? I definitely let it happen. She opened her eyes and said I shouldn't, she backed away and said she didn't want me to. But her clothing, her attitude told an entirely different story, I didn't know what to believe.

Do You blame me? Did I fail Your test? Did You know I would?

My heart is heavy and I can't sleep. All I think about is her, how I ruined her, how I ruined myself. How in one moment a world can be destroyed.

You knew I would fail yet You tested me anyways.

Rachel told the *shadchan*, he was appalled, said he won't set me up again, and even called my mother. My mother was appalled as well.

"*Oy vey*, no one will want to marry you if they hear."

I wonder if I'm even deserving of the wife I envision for myself. Certainly not anymore. Not even a girl like Rachel would take me at this point.

I know that everything is for the best and I should take this as a lesson to grow from but somehow I can't. I only see it as my downfall, my recognition of women as the *taiva* that they are, how they can hypnotize you in a moment and make you lose control.

Lose control for one moment and you're ruined for life— ruined her life.

I've asked her for forgiveness, even though she's partly to blame.

I'm asking *You* for forgiveness too, even though You set me up for failure.

Such close proximity, I really didn't mean it. I really didn't mean to reach across the gears and for a moment, just that moment, hold her hand.

My Parents Knew His Parents

My parents knew his parents. They went to the same fundraisers and bar mitzvahs, with overlapping friend circles. He was a boy from the neighborhood after all.

"Such a wonderful boy," my mother said, "Miriam says he helps out around the house—he sweeps the floors after the Shabbos meal. You don't know how important it is to have a husband that helps out." She smiled at my father tightly.

My father ignored her, "They also just donated a new *Kesser Torah* to the *shul*. Must have cost a thousand dollars, maybe two."

It was settled then, I'd go out with Ari Cohen.

Our first date was standard. He looked okay, a little scrawny, but well dressed. And he seemed well thought out too:

"I'm not into all these modern thoughts and ideas," he said, "women don't understand their place anymore, I even heard that those secular women let their leg hair grow out long," he took a deep breath, "at least you Orthodox women have more sense."

I thought of my silky shaven legs and sighed in relief, even though it was hidden under pantyhose and under the table. Sometimes I'd forget to shave for a few days. All my married friends, grimacing as my spikey leg brushed against them, would tell me, "don't worry, once you're married you'll remember."

At least my eyebrows, the part of me he could see, were definitely tweezed and preened to perfection, I never let them get out of hand.

"It really grosses me out," I agreed.

At home, my parents gushed, "He said great things about you. This may be the one!"

17

Our second date was pleasant, if but a bit short. We got drinks again, in a lounge. I was just starting to get comfortable and remove my jacket when Ari looked at his watch and jumped.

"We gotta go, I'm so sorry. I didn't realize the time." He threw his jacket on and paid for our drinks at the counter. I followed close behind him, nearly tripping over my heels.

He strode onto the street, I was a few feet behind him struggling to keep up.

Once inside the lot, he disappeared completely. I walked down one row, trying to recall where he had parked, helplessly, earlier I had just let him open the door for me and lead the way.

Five whole minutes I walked back and forth in my heels. My feet killed, my head hurt and my eyes started prickling. That's it? He'd just leave me here?

Someone called my name.

I looked up.

"C'mon!" Ari called from down the row of cars, "what happened?"

I walked as fast as I could without getting too flustered and let myself inside the car.

"What happened?" I repeated his question, "what happened to you? You disappeared."

"I told you to come," he sighed, "and then I spent twenty minutes looking around this parking lot for you. Whatever, you weren't fast enough, we missed it anyway."

"Missed what?"

"The first hour has free parking," he shook his head, "it's fine, don't worry about it."

I was so furious, all I wanted to do was to go home and kick off these stupid heels, I burst, "So I'll pay." As I said it I realized I only had four dollars on me and I had no idea how much parking could cost.

He looked taken aback, "don't be silly."

Outside my house, he said goodnight and told me that he had a nice time. I nodded once and closed the door.

The next day my parents told me the news, "he really likes you! I didn't know this was going so well. Don't be scared to get excited." They grinned.

I wasn't scared of anything.

The third date we went to a cute café.

"Are you hungry?" He asked.

I hadn't eaten all day.

"Not really," I lied.

"Okay, great," he said and chose a salad from the menu. He told the waiter, "bring two plates with it."

The salad was nice and topped with fried mushrooms. I am allergic to mushrooms. I took a small forkful into my plate and picked out the mushrooms. Then I moved the lettuce to one side of my plate as we spoke, sipped water, moved the lettuce to the other side.

We spoke about our parents and siblings. I told him about my nieces and nephews:

"I don't connect as much to the babies, but once they're older I'm definitely their favorite aunt."

"You don't like babies?" Ari froze mid-bite.

"Of course I like babies!" I tried to fix my mess up, "I love babies. I just really get along well with kids, y'know?"

He nodded slowly, I could tell he was choosing his words carefully and I was sitting tight and nervous.

"I just want to make this clear," he started, "I want to have a big family. I want a wife that could handle that... y'know?"

On the spot, I nearly cried. What he said made sense, of course, he wanted a motherly wife. I had to be that motherly wife. So instead of crying, I nodded, "of course. I want a big family too."

He smiled at me and I exhaled with relief.

"How was it?" My parents asked when I got home.

I shrugged and went to the bathroom to take off my makeup, shower and shave my legs.

In the morning they answered their question, "it's going great!"

The next date we went out on a picnic. He told me to make something for the two of us to eat, a surprise, something yummy.

I stayed up all night preparing the basket, even glue-gunning little bows on the sides for decoration. My father thought it was overdone, my mother thought it was perfect.

What mattered was what Ari thought.

He took a bite of the sandwich and said, "This is good!"

I beamed.

"Did you bring more mustard?" He dug through the basket, giving up after a minute, his face falling into an unimpressed look.

Oy, how could I have forgotten extra condiments? It was such a basic mistake. He shook his head, said it was fine and we spoke about other things.

The next date he told me his parents wanted to meet me.

"When? Tonight?"

"Well, I'm sure you'd want to dress up a bit, no? You could meet them next time."

At home, my parents cheered.

"This really is the next step," My mother gleamed.

"When can we meet him?" My father asked.

The problem started after we met each other's parents. My parents loved him, his parents liked me and all of a sudden Ari wanted to speak about engagement. It was the next step after all. The thing was, and it was hard to admit until this point, I wasn't feeling as excited as I wanted to feel. Once in a lifetime decision and all that, y'know?

"This isn't good," my mother said to my father, "our daughter is confused." And to me, "It's normal to be nervous, but you can't always run away from commitment."

"She has to speak to someone, a dating coach will set her straight. Such a fine boy," he muttered to himself

Her name was Mindy and she lived fifteen minutes away—an hour with traffic. I sat in her cramped living room as she prepared tea for us.

"So what's the problem?" she said finally.

"I thought I'd feel more excited..." I told her about him, about all of our dates.

She paused thoughtfully, "it sounds like you have a good basis with him. Let me ask you, you think dating is going to be like the movies?"

When I didn't answer, she pressed, "You think you're going to magically fall in love?"

"No."

"Good, because that's just made up. It's called infatuation. It's not a Jewish thing. We believe that love grows with time."

I nodded.

"I won't tell you what to do, but I can tell you that people aren't disposable. A good connection doesn't always come around so easily."

Ari proposed to me the following Thursday, he said he found a woman fit to be his wife. At the engagement party, my parents said they found a boy fit to be their son-in-law.

I Learn Gemara

I waited in the lobby, struck with nerves. Sara was only the third girl I was dating. The first two went horribly, didn't make it past the first date, and I'm not picky. Talia was very overweight and Dini was straight up rude.

A girl entered through the revolving doors. She looked around the expansive lobby and I held my breath. She had her hair clipped back, low heels and a shiny skirt, she looked like someone I'd want to get to know.

Please be my date, please be my date, I begged Hashem.

She walked towards me, made eye contact.

"Sara?"

She nodded, I nodded and grinned.

Sitting across from me, I could tell she was just as nervous as I, it put me more at ease. I really didn't want to mess this up.

"Tell me about yourself," I leaned forward. My mother told me that was a good way to start, ask about her work, her studies:

"I'm graduating this year," she said, "I'm going to be an elementary school teacher. I really love kids."

I asked her what she likes most about the week:

"My favorite day of the week is Shabbos," she said, "it just feels so holy. I really feel more connected, do you also feel it?"

I nodded, what else? I asked her what she does for fun:

"I'm very close to my grandmother, we go out for lunch together every Friday."

Just like that, she convinced me. She was perfect, the kind of girl I was looking for.

"Tell me about you," she smiled. I noticed her pearl earrings matched her teeth, and I felt calm.

"Learning has always been my passion," I said, "I take it very seriously. You know it's my fourth year in the Mir."

"Wow, it must be hard to sit and learn for so many hours."

"You have no idea," I sighed, "but it's worth it. The best moments are when I feel like I really get something... and then I realize there's a whole deeper level to understanding."

She sipped her tea holding the cup between delicate, long fingers, adorned with a simple ring. And I couldn't wait for it to be the fourth date already so it would be appropriate for me to tell her how nice her eyes were, and how her smile made me smile too.

"You know I want to keep learning. I really feel like I'm cut out for it," I continued. She knew this, of course, I wrote it on my resume. She wrote on hers that she supports learning, ideally and financially. Both of her brothers-in-law and three of her brothers were full time in *kollel*.

"Tell me about it," she smiled, "what are you learning?"

I stared at her blankly, "Gemara."

She laughed and brushed some fallen hairs away from her eyes, "Of course. Which *masechta*, I mean."

"Oh," I laughed, wondering if it meant anything to her, "*Kiddushin*."

"No way," she exclaimed, "which *perek*?"

"*Sheni*," I squinted my eyes

"*Daf?*"

"*Mem aleph*." My old nerves stuck up. That was the *daf* I remembered at least.

"Wow, unreal," she said, "Now, I'm not super feminist but what do you think of *tav lemeitev tan du, me'lemeitiv armeilo*?"

I choked on my coffee, took another gulp to clear my throat, "um, what?"

"Do you really think women are more desperate to get married than men?"

I racked my brain, tried to remember the seder from earlier. The Beis Medrash, my *chavrusa* Naftali and I, what had we shmoozed about? Which *daf*??

I remember Naftali was telling me about his cousins in London, how they invited him there for a wedding and he was dying to go just for the food. That family once threw a bar mitzvah at the Waldorf and the food they served... Naftali never ate so much cow in his life.

"Definitely go," I told him, "your parents would buy you a ticket, no?"

But what about the *daf*??? What did we say about the Gemara?

"Um..." I said, "I actually didn't either really get that part...you know, it's the kind of thing you have to learn a few times. I didn't know you learn Gemara?"

"I have a group of women, we get together a few times a week..." she looked at me with pursed lips and searching eyes and my heart cracked and I wanted to hide.

"Very nice." I said.

She nodded, drained her tea.

I left my coffee untouched.

A few minutes passed, I asked her a question, she answered shortly. She asked me a question, there wasn't much to say.

"Well, it's getting late," she yawned.

"Yeah, I'm really tired." I looked at my watch, 9:30, "we should get going."

Anyways, I never wanted one of those modern, Gemara-learning girls. She wrote on her resume that she was *frum*...not Reform!

We decided unanimously that it wouldn't work out.

Letters to My Love

I said "yes."

What I really meant to say was, "can we wait a little bit? This went quite fast, I've only known you for three weeks and I really like you, I'm just not sure I'm ready to commit my life to you."

But you asked so nicely, smiling your sweet smile and we went out enough times to know... to know what? That it was good. To know that it was getting better each date, that we had the potential to create something beautiful... right?

Every day after was painstakingly regretful. It's not that I didn't like you, it's not even that I didn't love you. It's that I didn't know.

Since our engagement, you started saying, "I love you."

And I answered back, "I love you, too." Because what else could I say? That I wasn't sure? That some days after spending time with you I'd come home elated and some days I'd return broken with nerves, wishing I'd never met you so I wouldn't be in this Parve situation?

Because that's what we were, even in our most fiery, intimate moments. Parve. Like Shabbos dessert ice cream— nice to eat because it's sweet but everyone knows there are better options out there.

I wondered if you meant it when you said you love me, too. If you really loved me or said it out of expectation. We were supposed to love each other after all: we chose each other for life.

Remember that day we painted the apartment? I was going to call the engagement off that evening. What a horrible, terrible day.

I got so excited when you said, "let's paint the walls!" Got dressed in an old shirt and worn out skirt, ready to finally have a fun, comfortable day with you. These past weeks we'd spent so much time on wedding prep, we could barely focus on building our relationship.

We got to the apartment, giddy at the prospect of living alone, together, of *being* alone now, even though we technically weren't supposed to yet.

You mixed the paint, got out the roller and started painting the walls. I worked on details like around the light switches and where the wall meets the floor, losing my mind with carefully placed tape that didn't help the paint from leaking.

Let me tell you, it was *not* fun.

So I dabbed your arm with the brush. That's what we came here for—to talk, to play, to have fun. Your reaction alarmed me:

"Why did you do that?" You snapped and ran your elbow under the sink, scrubbing aggressively. You came back, dipped the roller in paint and splattered it across my shirt, thick heavy blobs. *Seriously???*

I was so angry I wanted to scream. Instead, I painted corners obediently and didn't talk to you the whole time. The silence was unbearable and I felt you fuming from the opposite corner of the room.

We didn't talk for two days straight, until Benny's birthday dinner. We sat next to each other and acted like a couple for your parents, for your little birthday brother, for your grandparents. You never mentioned painting the apartment again, and when I dropped dishes off with my mother two weeks later all the walls were done. Good. If you don't want to have fun, you shouldn't get me involved.

I didn't like that you got angry and emotional and happy and sad. So extreme, I wasn't used to it. Everything you felt, you let it show, and you let the whole world know.

"Can you bring more techina?" You asked the waitress, four separate times.

"Forget it," I whispered as you tried to summon her again, "you don't need it."

"I like techina," you said simply and stubbornly. Could you get any more stressful?

That time you found the bag of zucchinis at a bus stop and asked every single person standing there: "Excuse me, is this yours?"

"Can you please just leave it?" I begged the whole time, horribly embarrassed. No one claimed the zucchinis.

When we finally went out to eat after our date got pushed off because of work and appointments and errands, and you said to the waiter, "two coffees please."

"Why two coffees? Who's drinking the second?"

"You."

"I never have coffee before I eat," I said, irritated that after all this time you didn't know and that you didn't even care to ask.

It bothered me that you were such a charmer. You made my parents love you more than they ever loved me, it seemed. The second I mentioned any doubt they'd jump to your defense:

"Look, no one is perfect. He has so much good going for him, you have to focus on that."

"What a fine boy, he just wants to please you."

Not that I expressed doubt often. My mother and older sister were pleasant sometimes, at other times they were downright scary.

"You can't make up your mind! What are you, five or twenty?"

"We spent ten thousand dollars on the engagement party, your wedding dress, sheitel, the hall. If you wanted to change your mind you should have done it a month ago!"

So I sucked it up and smiled and sent out the invitations even though I wasn't ready. I called my friends and told them about you in utter confidence even though I was not confident. I called *you* and spoke to *you* in utter confidence. Would it be better if I had told you how I felt? Would it make a difference?

The wedding date was ever impending. We set it the farthest that was appropriate yet yours and my family alike asked why we'd set it so for so long from now. A full three months away.

I still had so many questions, as I did the first date. How do you act under stress? How are you with babies? Do you easily forgive or do you hold grudges? But it never came up. I hope you are forgiving. I hope you help calmly and lovingly with the babies. I hope you continue to learn and love Torah even though you hate restrictions but find them necessary.

I hope you can be there for me, emotionally and physically, when I know I need you and when I think I don't.

In good times and in bad times because we are bound to have both.

We were supposed to be seeing each other through pink lenses. The honeymoon phase. Why didn't I feel it? Why did our engagement feel like the worst period of my life to date?

I knew you but not well enough. It was an awkward stage for us, transitioning between strangers to lovers and we weren't quite anywhere yet so we didn't know how to act. I couldn't tell you everything I felt. There was no space for that.

I didn't know if you felt this uncertainty too. I hoped you didn't because it wasn't a good feeling, yet I hoped you did so that we were on the same page.

The week before the wedding we saw each other one last time, out in a restaurant and it was unbearable.

We had nothing to talk about, so you spoke about sports. I cut you off with a heavy sigh. An hour past and the second hour inched by.

The next time I'd see you, you'd walk me to the chuppah. I wanted to go home and curl in bed with a movie, instead, I sat across from you and we spoke about the weather, about the news, about the holidays, about the seasons, about food and drinks and people we knew, about things we didn't care about.

At least you didn't order me a coffee this time.

So what brings me to write this letter to you that I will never send, on our wedding day of all days? Perhaps to read back in ten years from now, five kids and much relief that I went through with this. Perhaps to read back in ten years, divorced and sad and alone, having proof that I should have gone with my gut feeling.

Mazal tov, to us.

The Difficult Search

These days it's hard enough finding a decent date. Sure, the resumes sound great and the references always rave, but my mother is a pro at weeding out what their comments really mean:

One was quiet—"that means she's depressed," my mother explained.

One was plain—"poor," my mother said, "or worse, ugly."

One girl looked pretty in the pictures—not that I was looking—but my mother shook her head, "she has short hair now. Donated it or something. That's not the kind of thing a *kallah moyd* does."

"What about the girl whose father is a doctor?" I wondered.

My mother dismissed the thought, "Her mother is a shlep. Auntie Chava knows her from shul."

One was a size ten—"that usually means size sixteen," my mother explained.

One had two more years left at school—"you want a finished product, trust me."

Finally, there was one girl that sounded decent. Her name was Ariella, had hair a few inches past her shoulders, a degree in occupational therapy, a father that worked in business—"Tatty knows his name, that means business is going well,"—and she wore a size 2. Ariella's friends liked her, they said she was positive, sincere and had a true *yiddishe neshama*.

"So I'll go out with her?" I said looking at her picture. She was really nice looking and I was pretty excited.

"I'll call one more reference," my mother said, "and then I'll set it up."

My mother called the girl's high school teacher and relayed the conversation with me afterward, ashen-faced.

It went like this:

"You didn't know? She has a medical condition... low vitamin D or something. I know she has a *heter* from a rav, but I still think you should know..." the teacher said.

"Know what?" My mother was concerned and for good reason.

"She doesn't wear pantyhose. I spoke to her about this, to maybe reconsider but she said she needs the sun for her skin, it helps with her condition... I don't know what to tell you, but it's the kind of thing that's important to hear beforehand."

My mother thanked her and told her that yes, this kind of thing is important and shouldn't be hidden. Nothing against Ariella, she must be a wonderful girl, it's just about the standards of a home we want to keep.

I took a deep breath and got over my disappointment. Hashem sets things up and takes them away, it's important to know it's all *miShamayim*. There are more girls out there.

My mother crossed another name off the list.

Scarecrow

I told my mother that it wasn't worth it, I'm not doing anyone favors. It's just wasting my time, and more importantly *her* time. I've always been respectful of a woman's time. I really don't want to blame my mother, but by the fifth time of her pressing me to give it a try because 'a friend suggested it' and she was embarrassed to tell that friend no, I didn't have much of a choice.

So, I buttoned my shirt, tied my shoes, and combed my hair until it stood just right—ready for my date with Ahuva.

She opened the door for me on the first knock, paused for an appraising moment at my outfit, and whispered, "You don't want to meet my parents, right?"

I laughed and shook my head, "nope"

"Good answer," she followed me out to the car.

I liked her immediately. She was cute and funny, knew what she wanted and said what she thought.

In the café, we joked about the couple sitting across from us, clearly on an early date as well but with fewer laughs and way more awkward pauses than us.

"What do you think they're talking about?" I wondered.

She shrugged and tried imitating their unanimated conversation, "I... uh... think that its important... to... uh... be a good person."

That had me thinking: "What is *really* important to you?"

We agreed on everything.

Schools to send our kids to:

Middle of the road, modern chareidi.

How many kids we wanted:

"A lot," I said.

"But not *too* many." She added.

"Exactly."

Army:

"Well... if they really want to serve I'm not going to stop them," she said.

"But rather not."

"Of course."

Even our ideal vacation:

"Somewhere sunny, where I don't have to move a lot."

I nodded, "with a beach. There should be a beach too."

"An island!"

"Totally." I grinned.

We left the café only when we noticed all the chairs on tables and our waiter with a mop. It was time to go.

"I had a nice time," I said when I dropped her off.

She got out of the car and waved, "I'll see you."

And at that moment, I really felt that we would, *should*, and that we had something good going.

My mother saw my smile when I came home and guessed it too, "aha, so you did like her in the end!"

It was the worst case scenario because I *really* did like her, but I told my mother again "she's really not my look."

Because already from the picture I had seen before our date I could tell—a *blonde!* Why was everyone setting me up with blondes? She was the seventh blonde I went out with (in total I had been set up with nine girls), even though I explicitly say, "I'm into dark girls." (Specifically the Colombian type if you ask me.)

"If you really like her it could grow on you," my mother reassured again, "and she really is a pretty girl."

So I went out again.

Date wise, it only got better. She told me about her siblings and the family trips they went on together, I told her about the night I stayed home alone during a blackout when I was little.

She told me that she was afraid of the dark too.

Looks wise, she really messed up this time. I thought the baggy sweater she wore on our first date was a 'trend' thing, a stupid trend she bought into once. The second date I realized how wrong I was. It wasn't a one-off trend. It was her 'style' choice. This time it was worse than last, her skirt nearly reached the floor, her jacket oversized, covering any possible hint of curve. She was slim, I knew that, and tall—again, not my thing, I'm more into short girls—but with her clothing, she just looked like a scarecrow.

After dinner, we walked around. The restaurant was on Ben Yehuda so it only made sense to walk around that area. Oy, I cringed, I wished we were somewhere more private.

Me with the walking *scarecrow*, I hoped no one I knew would see us, I straightened my back and tried to focus fully on *her*, on her words, on her face. The moments I looked into her startling blue eyes were the moments when everything was fine.

We bumped into a group of *her* friends, they eyed me approvingly. One girl, smiling too much my way asked Ahuva, "So... *this* is your brother?"

Ahuva laughed, "No, we're going out. Do we look alike?"

"Kind of. You have the same coloring."

Another friend winked and said, "Well, have fun,"

Ahuva rolled her eyes, "We *are* having fun, you don't have to tell us."

Thank God we didn't bump into anyone I knew.

Again, I dropped her off and told her that I had a great time, I wasn't lying. She agreed and said the words on my mind: "You know, I really feel comfortable with you. Like I could fully be myself."

There was a moment stretched tangibly between us, our eyes did that electric thing again and I waved before more electric things happened.

At home I relayed the date to my parents, where we went, what we ate, smirking when I remembered we already had the next date set. It happened by chance, I was just telling her about the cholent they started selling Thursday night's in certain Cofix's, I was very doubtful of it but my friends dragged me along, and you know what? It was actually pretty good!

Her eyes lit up and she said, "Let's do it. I'm so down."

Cholent, Thursday night, that girl was such a chiller.

My mother caught the expression on my face and smiled smugly. She was right, wasn't she? Looks really do grow on you... I could get used to Ahuva.

I thought of her giant jacket and frowned.

There were a whole two days until Ahuva and I planned to see each other again, a lot of time for contemplation. Well, there was a lot to contemplate about:

Personality- 10/10. Hands down, no question. Besides being fun and funny, I really feel like she gets me. Look, I'm a sensitive guy and I'm super deep. I need a girl that could take that. On our date I tested her, I asked her if she ever feels helpless, if she feels connected to Hashem. If she thinks about death, if she thinks about love and forever and if she's afraid of the future—

"Of course I'm afraid," she said, "Aren't we all? But sometimes you just have to dive in headfirst, daven and believe everything will work out, right?"

I nodded, she was a hundred, million percent right.

Now let's talk about her looks.

My sister saw her picture and asked me, "she's pretty... you said she doesn't wear heels though?"

I shook my head, regretfully, wondering if she could even pull off heels at her height. Most probably she'd reach my height and it would be even more awkward to walk next to her.

"Is she pretty?" I asked, taking the phone back to have a look at her picture.

"I think she's beautiful," my sister said, "but she has to be drop-dead gorgeous in your eyes, of course."

Ahuva had big eyes and a gentle splatter of freckles on her cheeks. Her smile was nice and straight. She looked kind of like the actress that played in the Hunger Games... I sighed, not at all my style. I always imagined myself with someone more like Gal Gadot's vibes, or, when I let myself really fantasize—Arianna Grande. Sleek dark hair and a gaze that smolders.

Another thing about Ahuva, something I wouldn't tell my mother nor sister, was that she was pretty flat chested. Now, I'm not into *huge* busts, but something more than nothing is preferable... if you know what I mean.

I really don't mean to put Ahuva down. She really does have everything else: kind—volunteers in the summer with cancer kids, smart—has a degree in bioinformatics or something of the sort and is starting her masters next year, she likes kids, has a great relationship with her family and even wouldn't mind owning pets (I don't specifically want a dog but I like to keep my options open.)

"Do you think she's pretty?" I asked my mother.

She sighed, "At the end of the day *you* are the one that has to find her attractive."

Ahuva texted me good morning and we texted the whole day through. Of course we went out again, and again and again. Cholent, bowling, pottery, eating. She still wore flats and our conversations still went great.

Her eyes, light as they were, really did grow on me. I liked how transparent they were like she wasn't hiding a thing. I wondered if she felt that way about mine. I wondered if she appreciated my shoes, even if she didn't care for her own.

She met my parents (they loved her), I finally met her parents too (they loved me of course).

It was getting pretty serious so my mother confronted the main block in our relationship. She spoke to the *shadchanit* about Ahuva's clothes, the *shadchanit* said she'll call Ahuva's parents and that I shouldn't worry, they'd sort the whole thing out.

The next date things were looking up. She came in a tight shirt, the one I only saw peeking from underneath that big jacket of hers, and a short skirt. It wasn't tight but at least it showed off her toned calves—calves I've never even glimpsed before.

Indoors she shed her jacket and I eyed her appreciatively.

"I like your shoes," I said and winked. I actually least liked her shoes out of the whole outfit. Short platforms, but it was a start to some height. Maybe she liked to start that way, first the horrid All-Stars from our first dates, and then move her way up—platforms, then wedges and eventually, ultimately, stilettoes.

As sculpted as her calves were now, I couldn't even dream of how they'd look in stilettoes.

"I like your shoes too," she said.

We looked down at my mahogany dress shoes.

It was the start of progress and then a few more dates on she started talking about rings and committing forever, diving in head first and all that.

Sitting with her, it sounded great, the home we'd build— modern yet homey in design, Torah values, no cable TV but occasional movie nights, *Mehadrin* chicken but for dairy *cholav stam* worked just fine—the life we'd lead, we really were heading in the same direction.

But afterwards, I envisioned the wedding in my head: walking down the aisle in my tailored tuxedo to a pale girl, she'd look like a ghost in her baggy wedding gown—do wedding gowns even come baggy? For every *chatan*'s sake I hope not—everyone's eyes on us, would they think we're a hot couple? Would they think I settled?

That's when I realized (again), "She's just *really* not my type."

My aunt was over, she always gave the best advice, "Do you like her?"

"Yes!" I said.

"So, what's the problem?"

The problem? Ten years from now, walking next to her and imagining someone else, someone with dark almond eyes and caramel skin... someone I would never have. I asked my aunt what she thought.

"You're twenty-one years old," she exclaimed, "why should you settle?"

I texted Ahuva that it's not going to work out, deleted our messages and told my mother, for the love of Hashem, please stop setting me up with blonde girls!

Piglet

I told my mother it wasn't worth it, I'm not doing anyone favors. It's just wasting his time, and more importantly *my* time. I really don't want to blame my mother but by the fifth time of her pressing me to give it a try because 'a friend suggested it' and she was embarrassed to tell that friend no, I didn't have much of a choice.

So I put on a dress, touched up my makeup, as if it needed touching up—all ready for my date with Shmuel.

He picked me up in a battered car. Watching him park through the curtains, I already knew. Opening the front door for him, looking him up and down just confirmed my thoughts.

Let me first explain where I'm coming from. A top priority for me in a man has always been good hair. I write it on my resume, I tell it to my friends, I circle guys hairstyles in magazines that I'd like my husband to have. It's not my fault, I call it childhood trauma. You see, my father is bald—totally and shiny, in a way no yarmulke can cover. It was a great source of embarrassment for me when my friends would sleep over for Shabbos and listen to his *dvar Torahs* at the meal, I'd imagine all the horrible things they were thinking: *'Ew, I've never seen a balder head in my life.'*

And now *this*. Shmuel was balding.

He cleared his throat and straightened his tie, "Hi, how are you?"

I thought of all the ways I could get out of this date, looking back wistfully at my cozy house. Nope, no way out. I smiled pleasantly—because maybe after I'd tell him no, he'd think of a handsome friend that would be good for me—and followed him out.

We went for sushi, I was surprised.

"This is a bit casual, no?" I said.

"Do you like sushi?"

"Yeah."

"So then it's fine." He said, "Unless you'd rather go somewhere else?"

I sighed, "No it's fine. I'll just get a tempura futomaki or something like that."

The sushi was good and the conversation actually flowed, it flowed best when I focused on holding my chopsticks and not on his face.

We covered all the basics: what our siblings did, who our parents were, and our top three best Purim costumes.

"Hands down my alien costume. I was all green with this huge silver cloak"

I looked at his bald head and imagined it painted green as well. I laughed, definitely a good costume for him.

"I love dressing up as a princess."

"I see that," he said.

I came home smiling, climbing the stairs to my parent's room where I knew they'd be waiting up.

"Ooh! It went well!" my mother cheered.

I looked at my father's bald head peeking out from the blankets where he slept soundly and said, "Tell the *shadchan* to forget it."

"What!" my mother exclaimed, "look at that smile. Forget nothing."

"He's really nice," I said, "but his look is just *not* for me."

It wasn't just his head. As I thought more, I realized it was his wrinkled clothes, his sneaker shoes, his beady eyes, his oily skin... his whole attitude really. I'm more into the tall, dark and handsome look. Those guys with yarmulkes balanced atop curly hair, designer jackets, polished Oxfords, and a sharp jaw. I wouldn't either mind eyes that switch from brown to green. I saw that on a guy in a movie and knew it's the type of eyes I'd love to wake up every day to.

"Are you *kidding*?"

I've never heard my mother so aghast.

"What?"

"You had a great time! You'd end it with him just because of how he looks?"

His arms were really hairy too. I noticed when he rolled his sleeve up to check his watch. I shuddered, "yes, Ma. Yes, I would."

She woke up my father to see what he thought of that. My father told me it's no excuse. I had to give it one more shot. I had to go out at least once more with bald, oily Shmuel.

I groaned.

The second date, he showed up at my door. His suit was different, that was the first thing I noticed. More fitted, and ironed too. Cute, he was making an effort. Now he resembled a dressed up piglet.

I almost felt bad for not dressing up. I left my heels behind and wore a top and skirt this time instead of a dress. It barely seemed like he noticed anyways, excited as ever to see me.

Oy.

We drove to Coney Island and walked on the boardwalk.

"It's good you wore comfortable shoes tonight," he said.

"Are your shoes comfortable?" He switched from his sneakers to loafers, not quite Oxfords but at least dressy.

He shrugged, "they're all right. I kind of thought you'd be more into them…" he trailed off shyly.

Duh. I nodded politely and told them they were nice.

As we spoke I realized our views and goals were quite similar:

"I like living in New York, but I kind of miss Israel. Would you ever want to live there?" He wondered.

"No." I said, "My whole life is in Brooklyn. Why would I ever leave?"

"Yeah, definitely," he said, "we have a great community here, we have everything we need."

We agreed on the schooling system:

"These Jewish schools charge a fortune. It's a shame because what can poor families do?" He said.

"Yeah," I said, "I guess they just work harder. Make it work. Who knows? It's more important that they go to a good yeshiva and get that education as opposed to spending money on... summer camp? Well, that's important too..."

"Hmm, I see what you mean."

I think we were also on the same page about the lifestyle we wanted:

"Do you like shopping?" I asked him.

"I'd be willing to shop, but it's not my favorite pastime."

"Not for fun," I laughed, "if I need a new dress I'm gonna have to buy a new dress whether I want to shop or not, no?"

"Of course."

He dropped me off and told me he's looking forward to seeing me again. I smiled politely like always.

"I'm not going out with him again," I announced as I walked through the door.

"Why?" My mother asked.

"He's ugly."

"Don't say that!"

I shrugged, "he is, I'm not lying."

One more date, my mother said, she'd meet him before so she could see for herself. I rolled my eyes heavenward and groaned, "why, Hashem, why?"

My parents met him for a few minutes and then we ate out. The last free meal I'd get out of this guy. I ordered a salad and ate a few bites. Halfway through I told him I was tired and sick and all of those excuses.

He looked concerned as he dropped me off, "you'll call me in the morning to let me know how you feel?"

"Sure." I lied, "thanks for tonight."

"*Refuah shelaima*, and thank you. I had a lovely time."

I went home and called my mother down.

"You see what I'm talking about?"

My mother looked confused.

"His face! I'm talking about his face." I sighed heavily and went to the kitchen to find food.

"What do you expect?" my mother's voice turned nasty, "you expect a movie star? A model? I think he's a nice looking boy."

"Yeah," my father came down to join the conversation, "I don't see anything wrong with him."

"Well I do," I picked out vegetables from the fridge and started cutting them up, "and I'm the one that's marrying him."

My mom paused, "you're what? Marrying him?" she grinned at my father.

"No!" I transferred the salad from the cutting board to a bowl and stalked up to my room.

I thought that would be the end of it, ha!

"The *shadchan* is on the phone," my mother said the next day.

I shook my head but she gave it to me anyways.

"Shmuel really likes you."

"That is very nice to hear."

"Your parents told me about your... problem. I'm sure we can work something out."

Hair transplant? I smirked.

"Give it another shot, things will start to look up."

"I don't think it's a good idea..."

"Oh," she said, "I already told him. You're free Tuesday night, right?"

I wanted to scream. Instead, I answered politely— because maybe she'd have a handsome boy to set me up with in the future—"yes, Tuesday night is fine."

We went out Tuesday and Thursday and the following Sunday and Tuesday again. Once again for my mother, once for my father, again for the *shadchan* and once for my married sister who heard about my dates and called me up:

56

"Do you think I thought Yoel was handsome when we went out?" She laughed, "It took a year for me to actually like how he looks. Now I think he's the hottest guy in the world. These things take time."

My sister was married and pregnant a year into knowing Yoel, only then did she realize he might be attractive. She was not one to give advice.

It was probably a friend, Tehilla, who gave the best advice. She was more modern and going out with a guy for a few months now, also a guy on the uglier side of the spectrum.

"Well, I really feel like I became more attracted once we..."

"What?" I pressed.

"Well, once we stopped being *shomer*. You see, there's so much more to do than just look when you're touching."

I nodded, now how would I bring that up with Shmuel?

We went out twice more before I brought it up, after another date that went standardly okay.

Shmuel scratched the back of his neck nervously as I explained that I wanted to see how our physical chemistry was before making any rash decisions, "are you sure?"

I shrugged, "we could try, see how it goes..."

"Okay."

We were in his car parked outside my house. He reached over and put his chubby hand on my arm and paused. It was sweaty. I wanted it off. He slid it up to my shoulder.

"How is this?"

"I think this is enough for one night," I breathed and let myself out.

Shmuel understood that as an agreement to go out again. I felt trapped, condemned to a life of baldness, to sons with balding genes on both sides. I wanted to cry.

"I don't want to go out with him," I told my parents again.

"You're being picky. When you're thirty-five and still not married don't complain to me," my mother told me.

"You don't want to give up on your *bashert*," the *shadchan* told me.

"Yoel knows Shmuel from yeshiva!" My sister told me, "He says Shmuel's a great guy. Definitely husband material."

The next date he wanted to kiss me and I told him I changed my mind, I want to be *shomer* until the chuppah—and beyond, I thought and didn't tell him.

The chuppah. Shmuel was happy I brought it up, he actually planned on talking to me about that today. Oh no.

"We're getting pretty serious."

Are we? I nodded.

"And I really enjoy spending time with you."

Cute.

That night in bed I imagined a hairy, fleshy, bald-headed body next to me and felt sick.

The following week he proposed and I crossed off the days on my calendar. One year, my sister said. That meant I had eleven months to go before I found Shmuel somewhat attractive.

My One True Beshert

Ben Miller was the most handsome man I'd ever laid my eyes on. The first time I saw him—at my best friend's engagement party—I knew immediately I wanted him.

"Who is that?" I caught Ruchie for a moment between her smothering relatives and the aggressive photographers.

"I'm sure it's one of Baruch's friends," she whispered back.

"So he's single?"

"I'll ask Baruch when I have the chance," she said before she was whisked away for another round of photos.

All party long I watched out for clues. Nope, none of the beautiful wigged women approached him and claimed him. He seemed free for the taking.

Ruchie got back to me a few nights later, only after she ignored my texts and calls.

"So, did you find out?" I pressed.

"Well…" Ruchie was hesitant.

"Well, what? Say!"

"Baruch says he's single… but he might not be your type."

"How in the world would your fiancé know my type?" I was angry. I met Baruch twice. Once at Ruchie's house for a few minutes and the second time at their engagement party.

"Well, he's very modern… and older. Baruch only knows him from work."

"How old?"

"Twenty-seven."

"That's great," I said.

"Seriously?" Ruchie said.

"What else? What else do you know about him? What's his name?"

She sighed heavily and finally gave it over, "look, I just told you what Baruch said because he knows him a bit better so you should take his word into account. His name is Ben Miller."

Ben. What a hot name, perfect for the tall blond stranger in the classy black suit.

"Tell Baruch to set it up."

"I'll speak to him, see what he thinks..." she didn't sound enthusiastic and it bothered me.

"What? You like feeling powerful and great next to all your single friends?"

She started saying my name in a controlled, even tone.

I cut her off, "Because that's how it looks from the outside. I'm asking you to help set me up with someone I think is actually a real potential and all you do is tell me that you will try—"

"—Okay, okay! I'll speak to Baruch. We'll set it up."

And that's the only way to get selfish friends to do things for you—you guilt them.

The next day Ruchie called back, she said, "He gave Ben your number. Good luck."

It took me three hours to prepare for our first date. One hour on my face, my makeup was impeccable. One hour on my hair, it looked natural and wavy, but it was a process getting it that way. One hour deciding which outfit to wear. I almost had a breakdown then and there, on the bed in tights clutching both dresses to my chest. I took a deep breath, chose one blindly, tried it on again and went with the other one.

Ben looked so effortless, I nearly cried. His hair was a wonderful, combed, wavy mess, deep eyes under dark eyebrows, a maroon shirt and a leather jacket. His pants were fitted and his legs were long. He smiled and of course, his teeth were movie star straight and white.

We went to a dairy restaurant with dim lighting that complimented his face perfectly. It accentuated his bone structure, making it more striking and defined.

I was nervous and shy but Ben was so talkative that within minutes I fell under the spell of his voice and felt right in place.

He was telling me about the Pesachs his family spent abroad. This year they were flying to a five-star hotel in Rhodes.

"My family is begging me to go," he rolled his eyes, "they do not get that I'm too old for this kind of thing, you know what I mean?"

No, I did not know. My family only ever did Pesach in modest hotels upstate. Anyways I said, "Yeah, like, you're an adult, you want to do your own thing."

"Also, maybe I'd consider… but seriously, Greece? The Dominican was fun, I loved the Algarve. Why can't they choose something like that again?" He shook his head, "my father gets paranoid if he knows he's missing out a good deal. But this is a vacation, I'd say spend a couple thousand more and have a great time."

He asked me where I like to travel to.

"Oh, I'm pretty simple," I laughed it off, "I like to go to Miami when I have the chance."

I went to Miami only once, back in high school with Ruchie's family.

"Miami is great," Ben agreed and I sent Ruchie's parents' a million mental brachos for letting me have that experience, even if I had complained of homesickness that whole week long.

We got our food and Ben paused, he turned to the waiter, "You made a mistake."

"Didn't you order ravioli?"

"I did," Ben stuck his fork into a ravioli, "but I specifically said I don't want cheese."

"Oh, I'm sorry sir. I can sort that out—"

"The thing is," Ben cut him off, "I'm out with someone," he nodded his head towards me, "my date already received her order and it will take another twenty minutes at least for my dish to be ready. Am I right?"

"Um... I'm sure we can sort something out." The waiter tapped his pencil against his notepad nervously and I felt bad for him. Ben could be intimidating if he wanted to. He's the type of guy that knew what he wanted and how to get it.

"Just fix my order," Ben snapped, "that's all you could do."

The waiter left and Ben sighed, "Honestly, they never get it right."

Half an hour later they brought out his dish without the cheese, along with a profuse apology from the manager, and a dessert on the house.

I had waited for his dish to come so my pasta was already cold. I didn't mind the cold pasta nor the wait, it just meant more time with Ben.

I've always wanted an assertive husband, not shy and afraid to speak his mind like so many other losers I've dated.

Ben liked me, he told me straight out before he dropped me off. He said he'll give me a call.

"I'll be waiting," I told him as I brushed my hand through my hair.

"I know."

Before our second date, I went shopping. My mom only gave me two hundred dollars so I had to go to Century 21. I got new shoes and a nice dress, it was knee length and skin tight—I knew Ben would appreciate the effort to look hot and I wouldn't want my good figure to go to waste on baggy clothes.

Our second date went better than the first, he eyed my dress and I flushed red and happy. Our third date went even better.

Dating Ben wasn't like dating any other guy. I've been on dates before, to standard cafés and okay activities like escape rooms, bowling, ice skating. Ben was extravagant. He liked the top floor of the Empire State building because it had a view of the whole city, he liked yacht trips along the river and Broadway shows. He also liked to buy me gifts, perfume from Macy's, flowers to my door.

I buried my face into my hands when I read the note that came with the roses:

'I could get used to buying you roses.'

For me the best part of our dates wasn't at the expensive shows or exclusive restaurants, it was sitting in the passenger's seat of his nice sports car. The passenger's seat—that's where a wife belongs, Ben said and I agreed. I looked sideways at his strong profile and felt so in place.

Ben didn't like the drives as much. He spent most of the time cursing out everyone else on the road, mumbling under his breath about horrid drivers and the places he'd like them to go.

It was cute, how he got so riled up. It was hot, the way he held the wheel so tight his muscles rippled.

"Don't worry," I told him, "we'll get there eventually."

"Shut up," he snapped, and then in a different tone, "Sorry. I just don't like when people tell me what to do."

I laughed it off.

Two weeks from our first date I could tell Ben was getting antsy. He wanted to kiss me... maybe even sleep with me.

I realized from the stories that Ben had told me, that he's had women in the past. Of course, he had. I exhaled heavily, how could someone with a body and a face like that not? The girls that he'd hung out with on his island getaways, the girls he'd spent nights with on his European ski trips. That was back when he was younger, he explained, back then, he didn't care much for religion. Now he's different, he's more mature and wants a proper wife and family.

My eyes shined when I heard that. I wondered if he noticed my eyelashes, they were fake and long but natural looking.

But there would be moments when he'd hold my hands or grab my arms and look me so deep in the eye, straight down to my soul.

It was almost impossible to say no. Ben knows how to get what he wants, and he has full perfect lips to go along with it. But I'd shake my head and pulled my hands free.

Staying *shomer*, my mom told me, is the only way to get a guy to marry you. If not, they'll just use you up and throw you out. Then they'll find someone pure—it's easier for guys—and you'll be stuck. No one would ever marry you if they knew, nobody wants a used girl.

That was part of the reason I said no, the other part was because I was so terrified I'd be a horrible kisser and he'd leave me mid-kiss. Roll his eyes that way he did and curse me out like the other drivers on the road.

"Maybe I'll go to Rhodes," he mentioned once, "if you come with us."

I laughed, unsure if it was a joke or for real. Pesach was three weeks away and we weren't even engaged. What would his parents say, what would my parents say?

He shrugged, "the last time I brought a girl they didn't mind."

I almost said yes, but I took a deep breath and told him how I really felt, "I wouldn't feel comfortable going, unless we were engaged."

"Engaged?" He said taken aback, "engaged." He repeated, testing the word.

"Don't you want to get married?" I said and blushed, it sounded like I was asking him if he wanted to marry me, "I mean... don't you ever want to marry?"

"Of course," he said, "I just thought you're young. Maybe you'd want to take some time."

"I'm twenty-one." I said. He nodded and I explained because he didn't understand all the nuances of shidduch dating, "I'm a girl. That means I'm practically ancient."

"What does that make me?" He smirked.

"It doesn't matter how old you are, because you're perfect."

"Am I?"

And we both laughed because we knew it was true.

I looked at his lips and smiled, imagining those lips on our kids. We'd make the most beautiful babies, they'll have golden hair like him, my green eyes and his full lips.

A few dates later Ben brought up how maybe it's time to meet each other's parents. I smiled so big on the inside because it meant my plan was working, my plan on getting Ben to propose. Each date I wore a new hot outfit, something tight, or slimming, or red or bold, nice heels and flattering but different makeup styles. It was important to keep things fresh, to keep him wondering and wanting. I didn't let him touch me and I knew my mother would be proud... even though I never mentioned any of this to her. She'd go on about how inappropriate it was and how I shouldn't go out with him if he insisted like that. Well, now she'd meet him for herself, see his lips and understand my struggle.

Ben dressed up for the meeting. He wore the suit I remembered from Ruchie's engagement party and said all the right things.

"You have a lovely home," he told my mother, and to my father, "I didn't fully understand what kind of business you do?"

We sat in the living room. Maria, the cleaning lady, spent four hours shining the wood and fluffing the pillows, but I felt she could have worked harder. I baked brownies for the occasion. It was a huge fight between me and my mother because she didn't want crumbs on the floor. Maria just cleaned, and she wanted it to last until Pesach.

"So, sell the floorboards!" I told her and made the brownies anyway.

Dani, my baby brother—he's actually eight but he's still my baby—walked into the room. It was after nine p.m., he was supposed to be in bed, I wanted him out but smiled warmly because what could I do? Ben was watching.

"Dani!" I said, "Did you meet our special guest?"

"Hi," Dani said and went for a brownie.

"No!" My mother yelled but he grabbed one anyways, spinning to dash with it from the room. He bumped into Ben's knee and tripped over him. The brownie fell onto the floor, splattering crumbs on the rug and between the cracks on the floor.

My mother groaned. Ben cursed and the whole room went silent. Ben cursed again, quieter this time. I turned to tell him to *"shhhhh, we don't say those words in this house and especially in front of Dani,"* but then I saw Ben's pants and nearly cursed myself. Brownie smeared across his thigh in a horrid streak.

"Oh no," I jumped up, "I am sorry, I am so sorry."

"Get me a tissue! Get me something," he demanded.

Of course, of course. I dashed to the kitchen for a clean towel and seltzer.

Ben wiped it and it actually looked much better, the brown fading into the black of his pants. He didn't look completely pleased but said, "It's fine, I'll just take it to the cleaners tomorrow."

Afterward, he thanked my parents for a nice time, they thanked him. As soon as he was out the door, they turned to me. My father started, "How can I say this?"

"Say what?" I demanded.

"Don't you think he overreacted a bit about his pants?"

"Not at all," I said finally and went to sleep before they could argue over more stupid details.

The following week, Ben took me on a romantic boat ride and insisted again, "I really want you to come to Rhodes."

"I told you..."

"I know," he smiled and reached into his pocket.

The ring was gorgeous. He was even more gorgeous, smiling so whole and happy. And mine.

"We're engaged now," he said and pressed his lips to mine before I could stop him.

I pulled apart and looked around to see if anyone was watching—*or chas v'shalom*, someone I knew. The whole deck was empty.

I smiled nervously at Ben, he still held my arms and they felt numb like they'd fall off.

Oh no! I froze. His lips were stained pink from my lipstick. I covered my mouth and ran to the bathroom to reapply before he could see how thin my lips really were.

"I'm sorry," he said on the way home, "I shouldn't have done that without your permission."

"It's okay," I said holding my engagement ring closer for inspection. We were getting married anyway.

I thought the ring would shut them up, my parents didn't stop:

"I don't know how to tell you this. You really seem to like him."

"—I love him," I interjected.

"But you're not realizing the whole picture."

"What are you saying?"

"I don't think he's good enough for you. I think you deserve much better. You deserve a boy with good middos who will always treat you well."

"I deserve a *man*," I stressed, "like Ben. He's perfect and treats me like a queen."

"That's why he screamed at your little brother?"

"His suit cost more money than Dani is worth!" I shot back. That's what this was about? It was my punishment for baking those stupid brownies in the first place.

Ruchie called me up, "I heard you deserve a mazal tov?"

"Yes." I smiled.

"That's so nice!" She said and I could tell her tone was forced. Halfway through pleasantries she broke, starting with a heavy sigh and the real reason she called, "I spoke to Baruch again. He really doesn't think it's a good idea. They've been working together for over a year and he says Ben's not the most trustworthy guy..."

I tuned her out as she spoke, thanked her when she finished and hung up.

Women have intuition. It says so, in the Torah, we have this *binah* that lets us know when things are good and when things are not. I knew Ben was my bashert from the moment I set eyes on him at the engagement party.

The next few months flew by. I went to Rhodes, found a wedding dress—my mother paused before putting the deposit down, "are you sure?"—booked a hall grander than I'd ever dreamed of marrying in.

The chuppah was beautiful, dripping with flowers. I barely noticed. I had my eyes on Ben. The tall, handsome man with fine lips that twisted upwards into sweet smirks.

My parents walked me down the aisle, pulling me back every step of the way.

In the yichud room, Ben kissed me like he never kissed me before, held me against the wall so hard it hurt, his fingers digging bruises into my thin arms. He squeezed me tight and bruised my lips because he loved me and wanted me.

"I'm sorry," he said.

"It's fine," I said and reapplied my lipstick.

Game Over

It was the third date with Shaina and I was excited. The first went great and the second only went better.

Shaina was different, she was cool.

We went bowling and of course, she was cool with that.

We took up our lane and I chose a nice heavy ball. She contemplated between a bubble gum pink and an orange one.

I was up first. I aimed at the center and twisted twenty degrees left. My ball hit eight pins down and I grimaced. I was aiming for worse. My mom said I should go easy on the girls, it's not nice to be a show-off. I threw the second ball to the gutter to compensate.

"Nice!" Shaina said as my score appeared on the screen. She, of course, chose the girly pink ball.

"I come here a lot," I mentioned so she wouldn't feel bad. I hadn't gone bowling since my last third date with a girl, four months ago, and that girl asked for bumpers mid-game. Oy, embarrassing.

Shaina scrunched her face as she concentrated. She hit a few pins on her first throw, knocked the rest down on her second. Spare.

I brought drinks to celebrate, flavored water for her and cola for me. We sat and watched other bowlers for a bit.

"It's interesting," Shaina said, "there's a whole bunch of activities like this that just exist for entertainment."

"What else would activities be for?" I wondered, and "It's important to have fun in life, isn't it?"

"Definitely, but I don't know if that's the main thing..."

"So what is?"

"Fulfilling whatever purpose we were put here for," she said, "and if we're doing it right then I think fun comes along with it."

"What do you mean?"

76

"Hmm," she thought, "you love accounting, right?"

"Sure." I liked how it paid at least so it wasn't lying.

"So, you doing your job is you fulfilling one of your purposes and enjoying it too."

"I see. So right now," I said getting up and choosing my ball, "I am fulfilling my purpose of getting to know you better. And we're having fun with this lame, entertaining sport as we do it... right?"

I winked and she laughed. I liked her laugh.

I bowled worse this time, on purpose. She got a strike.

"That's amazing!" I cheered her on.

The following round I let myself do okay, I couldn't let myself fall too behind. Shaina got another strike.

This time I aimed for the center, no need to go easy. I could allow myself a strike as well, at least to be even with her. The ball rolled directly down the middle. It knocked eight pins down. The second hit nothing.

Next round: She got seven. I got two.

Next round: She got a strike, I got a spare.

Then she hit eight, I got three.

"You're really good," I told her.

"I am, right?" She grinned, "Bowling isn't lame at all, it's great."

"I'm glad you see the light," I said and prayed to Hashem for a strike. Gutter ball.

She took her turn and I glowered at her perfect form, her mechanical yet graceful aim. Wait—she wasn't turning her wrist right, I realized. So her form wasn't as perfect as she thought. Should I tell her? Was it rude?

I mentioned it in the passing.

"Oh," she scrunched her nose as she thought, "my bowling teacher used to tell me otherwise."

"I didn't know you had a bowling teacher." Why would she keep that from me? To make me look stupid as I let her win?

She laughed, "I told you my friends and I were obsessed. We really were ridiculous," she rolled her eyes, "we wanted to make a bowling team so we got together and had a teacher for two or three lessons. Not that we ever made a team, of course."

Shaina tested her aim, focusing on her wrist and bowled a strike. She shrugged, "should I show you how she told us to hold our wrist?"

"I'm fine," I grumbled, trying to imitate her wrist angle from memory. My ball dove to the gutter.

The game dragged on. I was bored halfway through, so bored that I didn't even try. I just let her win the rest to feel good.

"That was fun," she said as we left the bowling alley, she was the loosest and talkative I've seen her, and it was unnerving, "maybe I'll call my friends and we'll go out for a game for old time's sake." She looked at me and at this angle, I noticed her big nose, "thanks so much. I really had a great time tonight."

"Yeah," I said, digging my fists into my pockets, "It was nice."

"I'm sorry if—I don't know—you're sad or something..."

"Why would I be sad?" I snapped.

She shrugged and scrunched her face that way that she did and it made her nose resemble a shriveled raisin.

I don't like how she assumed things about me, I hate when people do that...and honestly, thinking further, there were a lot of things I didn't like about her. On the first and second date, she hid them well but now it was all coming out. It's the reason bowling is recommended for daters—see your date in other scenarios than just sitting. Well now I've seen it all: Shaina is sly, sneaky and competitive.

Definitely not the kind of girl I'm looking for.

Working with Them

We worked in the same office for a year. It dealt with international kosher delicacy distribution. I worked with sales. She did logistics. At first, we'd only nod at each other when we arrived at the same time. And work stuff. She'd print my papers, I'd email her receipts. But then we'd exchange a few words before heading to our desks. It was dangerous, I knew. It was dangerous and I still found myself slacking on work duties and looking up when she passed by... only to find her looking too.

And then one day we ate lunch together. It happened by chance and it was wrong but no one was watching. We went to the same sandwich place a few minutes from work and there was only one table available. It only made sense. It only made sense to talk, to ask her about her preferred sandwich topping, about her family, about her friends, about her goals and dreams. She was twenty and pressured to get married. She didn't say as much but I could tell by the way she answered.

"You'll continue working here next year?"

"I hope not."

"What do you mean?"

She shrugged and said mysteriously, "maybe something will come up and I'll have to quit." Marriage. Then she'd have babies, her next full-time job.

I was also pressured to get married. Since I quit Yeshiva and started working at this job my parents told me I was limiting my chances. No one wants a working boy anymore. I didn't believe them but here I was, a year later and still single. Almost twenty-two. When my father was my age, as he keeps reminding me, he had two kids. I was falling behind.

I finished my sandwich, got up, and realized she was still in the middle of hers. I half paused, almost sat, stood back up, wondered what to do. She noticed my stumble and said dismissively, almost embarrassed, "I'll see you."

Of course. I was embarrassed too. This was a girl from work, I shouldn't be engaging in such leisure conversations with her. The whole walk back to the office I felt grimy with guilt.

A few nights later, my friend Shlomo called:

"I got a job."

"Mazal tov!" I wasn't surprised, Shlomo was also more modern like me, always fidgety throughout *shiur*. He was single and had stayed in Yeshiva until now for *shidduchim*, not that it did him any well.

"I'm scared though. The job is in a mixed environment. I'm thinking of dropping it. I don't know what to do."

"My office is mixed," I told him.

"I know, that's why I'm calling you. What do you do?"

"What do you mean? I don't do anything…"

"You're with *them* all the time. How do you keep yourself from talking to them?"

"Well…" I thought of my lunch with Dini and the guilt returned, even stronger because the memory was laced with a dangerous sort of pleasure, "The main thing is to keep things professional. Only say what you need to say. You shouldn't run into trouble that way."

We spoke a bit more, Shlomo thanked me and hung up.

I spend the evening thinking of Dini, so modest and soft-spoken, her skin glowed with a gentle beauty. The kind of beauty that grows on you the more you stare. One year was long enough for the beauty to drive me crazy. If that girl didn't get married and quit soon I was scared I'd go completely mad.

"Did you hear of Dini Gold?" I asked my mother innocently over Shabbos.

"No," my mother said, "why?"

I shrugged. I couldn't tell her that she was a girl from work. It would mess everything up. She'd make me quit and go back to yeshiva. This wasn't how good *bochurim* met girls. They met through a *shadchan* and only through a *shadchan*.

"She's my friend's sister. Maybe ask the *shadchan* to set us up." I mumbled the last part.

"Whose sister?"

I froze and went to my room, positive my mother read through me. I didn't bring it up again.

What do I do about *them*? Shlomo's words continued to echo in my head. Well, I pretend they don't exist even though *they* are so present as I try to focus on the charts on my screen. So present as I cross the hallway for water and see pink lipstick staining a cup.

So present as I type notes. She passes by and I look up. She goes down the hall to the bathroom. A few minutes later she passes by my office again, without even turning her head.

What do I do about *her?*

I'd like to call it chance that I ended up by the sandwich place again, a moment after Dini entered. It wasn't chance though, I followed her and sat by her table.

"It's a nice day today, isn't it?"

The sky was grey and it drizzled, but so far so good. And I was talking to Dini, even better, sitting across from her and it was okay and casual and I wasn't doing anything wrong. Nothing unprofessional in talking about the weather.

"I like the rain," she said.

"You know, most people like sunshine more," I said.

"But the rain is more mysterious," she said, "it's more interesting."

And we spoke again, about more interesting things— places we've visited on summer vacation and places we'd like to visit. About inspiring people that changed our lives and people we'd like to meet. We spoke all lunch break long.

Afterward, we walked back separately. I left a few minutes after her, spent an extra-long time *benching* to spare any awkwardness. We didn't speak for the rest of the day. Professional environment. She faxed me papers that I filed away.

The following day I followed her to lunch again, sat with her and spoke and grew more and more intrigued by what she had to say.

Her favorite color was blue.

She loved to sing.

Her younger sister was getting married in May and she asked Dini's permission and Dini said it was okay and pretended not to mind for her sister's sake.

Lunch became a habit. Eating, laughing, talking, and walking back separately.

She liked listening to me too. I told her about leaving yeshiva, how it was a big deal for my family but I wanted to do what was good for me, regardless of what anyone else said. I still go to *minyan* every day, still learn sometimes and still love Torah of course, I assured her.

Meanwhile, I went out. I was in *shidduchim* after all. Most of them were just first dates, with cute girls that didn't have much to say. Not many made it to the second and barely to the third.

Dini must also be going out, I thought. How many dates did she go on? She could be up to her eighth date with a boy for all I knew. I'd have to wish her 'mazal tov' soon, for all I knew, burning inside as I'd say the good wishes.

Dini's dates. It started as an innocent musing. And all of a sudden I could think of little else. When she came to work dressed extra fancy and her eyes more sparkly I'd think—tonight? Is she going out tonight? I'd think of who it could be. If it was someone I knew. If it was a friend of mine. That would be the worst, for Dini to end up with a friend of mine.

I pushed it off for a week. The itching question. The itching, burning question that would ruin me if this didn't go well, but I didn't know how else to go about it. I had to ask her out. Unprofessionally and completely socially unacceptable.

I waited through the full burning day until lunchtime. At the counter, Dini asked for her sandwich to go.

"Do you want to sit for a bit?"

"I've actually been meaning to speak to you about that."

"So let's sit and discuss," I smiled.

We took our usual seats and it felt natural and normal to sit with this girl and the grimy guilt that used to loom, recently took a backseat. *That's the* yetzer harah *winning*, a voice hissed from inside. Worse still, I barely minded.

"Dini—"

She said my name at the same time.

"You go first," I urged.

She took a deep breath and said it: "this is wrong. We can't continue like this. I'm not the kind of girl that just schmoozes with boys. This isn't leading anywhere good and I... I'm sorry," her voice faltered, "I'm sorry. I don't know how else to tell you."

I nodded, "you're right."

I stared at my sandwich and the lettuce peeking out. It didn't look so appetizing anymore.

"What did you want to say?"

"About the same thing," I said offhandedly.

She laughed lightly and said, "Good we're on the same page." And took her sandwich to go and I sat alone and it felt wrong facing her empty seat.

I should've asked her out anyway. No, she wouldn't have gone out without going through a *shadchan*. She was good—too good and kind and righteous and it hurt.

Who am I? A yeshiva drop out? This couldn't lead anywhere good.

The next few weeks were murder. Every time she'd pass my office, on the way in or out. Or to the bathroom. Or to another office. Or anywhere. Any move. I was hyper aware and put my head down and pretended not to be, engrossed in work instead. Sure.

The papers on my desk from her desk—I'd search them for clues, for some sort of note she'd never leave. I send no note back.

I didn't think of her on the dates I'd go on with other girls. I didn't think of her on my first date with Hindy, how she was smarter than Hindy. Or on my date with Leora, how she was prettier than Leora. Nor with Chanie—she was sweeter than Chanie. I even went out with another girl named Dini. There was no comparison.

And then it happened, not two months later and Dini stopped showing up. An empty desk and I told myself she was sick. A few days later a guy moved into her office.

"She quit." A co-worker said.

Onto her next full-time job.

Word to the Wise

Dating scared me, from reading the resumes and judging people off a piece of paper to the dates themselves, first impressions, top behavior and the painstaking wait of hearing back: Did it go okay? Do they like me?

I've always been confident, about my looks, my personality, but after getting turned down so many times I felt a little crushed. It was better to be less controversial and opinionated, I realized.

Nesanel Friedman didn't turn me down. We went out once and the date was short but it went great. He laughed at my jokes and even made me laugh, telling me about the yeshiva *latkas* he avoided—so oily you could put a wick in and it lights for eight days.

The second date went even better. We had more in common than we thought:

"I have a mat in my dorm room," Nesanel said, "I do yoga every day."

"That's amazing!" I said, "I *love* yoga. I go to these awesome classes in the gym."

"So what do you eat after you work out?" He asked, genuinely curious and I was touched.

"I try to go for plant-based proteins."

We compared our diets, explaining each component.

He tried avoiding food colorings and sodas. I told him I avoided soup made with soup mix and ketchup induced cholent.

"Wow, that's really hard," he sounded impressed.

"When I go to a *kiddush* there is literally nothing for me to eat." I agreed.

"It's really fun talking to you." Nesanel told me on the way home, "I wish we could stay out longer, but it's just the second date... my Rabbi already thought our first date went on too long."

"It's okay," I said, holding back my smile—he must *really* like me, "there's always next time." I've never said that on a second date, but he seemed so positive it got me excited.

Our conversation deepened on our third date at a healthy salad restaurant.

"Sometimes I'm too hard on myself," I told him, "but I always feel like I have to move forward. I want to live the best life I could lead."

"If we're not going up, we're going down," Nesanel nodded, "I'm also hard on myself but I try to remember we're human. We're bound to mess up, and it's okay. What's important is to learn and accept... I think it's the only way to move forward."

"Yeah," I looked up and noticed his eyes. They were brown and deep and made my nerves tingle. An endless second passed between us and he looked away.

"Anyways, I'm happy you're telling me this. My Rabbi said if your skirts are that short then you're not for me, but I told him you are willing to grow. I could tell."

I looked at my legs under the table, my face growing red and hot. I was wearing a black pencil skirt. I got it with my mother. In the dressing room we did all the tznius tests: not too tight on the tush, covers my knees when I stand, when I sit. We had our seamstress sew up the slit. What did I wear on the last date? On the first date? How did his Rabbi know what I wore? Did he see us? Did Nesanel tell him??

I continued the conversation as evenly as I could, "of course I'm willing to grow. I *am* growing… in fields that are important for me to grow in." His Rabbi couldn't know how much *chesed* I did, or how much *tzedaka* I gave and that I was trying to do and give more.

"Of course! And you should only change when you're ready."

At home I asked my mother, "is my skirt too short?"

"You want to look like a woman or a bag?"

I chose my outfit carefully for our next date, a longer dress cinched at the waist with a belt. A nice compromise, I thought.

We went to the same salad place as last time.

"I want to go somewhere that you'll have something to eat," he explained.

"I don't just like eating, you know."

"Well, what else could we do?"

I thought he was joking but he didn't laugh, he genuinely didn't know.

I shrugged, "we could do an activity. Bowling, ice skating, the zoo." I thought of other dates I went on but then I felt weird like I was telling him where I expected him to take me and pay for me, "we could also just walk around. Go to a garden, a park..."

"Wow, that all sounds nice," he smiled and my heart melted. His smile was really cute, it showed off his chipped front tooth and made his eyes sparkle. I didn't ask him how many girls he went out with before me but I had a feeling I was his first. He didn't know all the 'rules' so of course, he had to ask around.

We ordered salads and spoke about reaching our full potential.

"That's why I love being in Yeshiva," Nesanel said, "I feel like each day I excel. I'm in an environment where everyone is dedicated to working harder, becoming better."

"That's why I love my gym!" I said and laughed at the comparison, "really! From week to week there really is a physical difference. It makes me feel like anything is possible, all you need is to do something steady."

"You go to a gym?"

"Yep, with my mom."

He went silent and thoughtful. The face he wore while contemplating was even cuter than his smile, I decided. He'd squint his eyes and bite his lip—

Nesanel opened his eyes wide, "oh no. I'm really sorry."

I jumped, "what? What happened?"

"I didn't realize, do you see that?" he started to get up.

"What?"

The *hechsher...*" and he was gone.

I looked at the *hechsher* framed on the wall near the kitchens. Glatt Kosher. Nesanel brought a waiter over to the *hechsher* and gestured towards it, asking him something. A man in a suit came—the manager? Nesanel spoke to him for a few minutes, stepped outside speaking into his cell phone.

He was out for at least twenty minutes. During that time a waitress brought our food. My salad looked so good, topped with sweet potato and chopped nuts. I picked one piece with my fingers and pushed the rest aside to wait for Nesanel.

Finally, he came back, "I'm really, really sorry."

"What happened?"

"The *hechsher...* it expired a month ago. I spoke to my rabbi about it, he said we shouldn't eat here."

"Nesanel!" I sighed and rolled my eyes, "I know this restaurant. The owner is a family friend. It's fine, really."

"I said I spoke to my rabbi," he said, "he advised me against it."

I looked away from my tempting salad, wishing I'd picked at it more. He paid, left a tip and we left.

"Well, now we can walk around," he said lightly and then paused, "look, I'm really sorry. I feel really awkward about what just happened. Could we just... forget it and have fun?"

"Yeah, don't worry, I understand where you're coming from. It's fine, really."

We walked around and went to a park and sat on a bench and spoke to a backdrop of glowing street lamps. It was fun and romantic and Nesanel told me we should sit a little farther apart even though he really wanted to sit closer.

"It was a mistake, I'm sorry," Nesanel said on the next date.

"You apologize too much," I said. Even though apologizing was sweet and he really was genuine about it. I wasn't sure what he was even apologizing about.

We were at a restaurant again. A meat one with a good *hechsher* and not much for me to eat on the fatty menu.

"My rabbi said it's not appropriate. We're supposed to talk *tachlis*. Everything else we could do once we're engaged, married."

"What do you mean, 'everything else'?"

"Activities. Even sitting in the park. It's not the kind of thing we should do."

"I've been out with fifteen guys and went bowling with all of them." I took a deep breath to calm down, regretting telling him how many guys I went out with. It would make him wonder what's wrong with me, why I'm not married yet.

"Well I'm not all the other modern guys you went out with." he shot back, "I have standards and I want to keep to them."

"No problem, keep your standards." I folded my arms and ordered a tea, even though I was hungry. This was getting ridiculous, Nesanel was treating me like I was barely religious. I have standards too.

I brought it up with him.

"I don't get it," he said, "don't you want to be the best Jew you could be?"

"Of course I do!" I said, "I just..." Just what? I'm lazy? No. Didn't believe? *Chas v'shalom.*

We spoke on the phone that evening. It was our first phone call and it lasted forever.

"We spoke for three hours!" Nesanel realized. He sounded regretful.

"Don't worry," I told him, "we spoke *tachlis*."

We really did. We spoke about our childhood, the parts we loved and would like to recreate, the parts we disliked — "we don't have to talk too much about the negative." Nesanel said and I agreed.

We went out twice a week but spoke on the phone every night.

"It's fine," I told him, "we're getting to know each other better."

Our phone calls were somehow more intimate than our dates ever were. We couldn't hold eye contact over the phone, but we could speak more openly and comfortably. Where our dates ended with Nesanel regretting our intimacy and blinking away from our electric eye contact, on the phone he would tell me he misses me and likes me and likes where this is going and wants to be with me more and more and sees me in his future and hopes I do too. On the phone, he told me that he loves me.

"I want you to be real with me, always," I said.

"I'm trying," he said, "I really am. I just want to do the right thing."

"Can we please go out together during the day? Somewhere fun. We could go to the beach."

"The beach?" He was taken aback.

"In regular clothes!" I laughed, "Just for a change of scenery."

The beach was a bad idea, we compromised with the botanical gardens. We spent all of Sunday walking through roses, with sandwiches Nesanel prepared for us—whole wheat bread and lots of vegetables. It was such a kind gesture, I didn't tell him that I generally don't eat bread. I ate the whole thing. We watched the sunset over cherry blossoms and felt the night grow chilly, sitting close on a bench, so close his leg brushed against mine. It felt natural and warm and I looked up into his eyes.

Nesanel jumped up, shaken, "I'm sorry. I'm sorry. I'm sorry."

"Stop apologizing!"

That night he told me he wanted to marry me.

The next day he changed his mind (kind of):

"My rabbi says you're a bad influence on me," Nesanel whispered so I pressed the phone to my ear, "I told him you really are growing. I really want this to work out, you don't know how much I want this to work out. Can you just go to a shiur once a week?"

"What?"

"He wants to see that you're growing. I told him you are but he says it doesn't just happen… and I agree. You have to work towards it. You once said yourself, you only see growth if you keep steady. That's why you go to that goyish gym of yours."

"I *am* keeping steady," I said. I ended the phone call curtly and told him I need a lot of time to think. About us, about where this was going, about if this was going anywhere at all.

He called me back and gave me no choice, "we really have something special. Don't you see it? Don't you feel it?"

"I do, but I can't be in a relationship with you if I feel like you're always trying to change me."

"I'm not trying to change you. I'm being open with you about things that bother me. You'd rather I keep it to myself?"

"Oh," I laughed, "so I should tell you everything about you that bothers me?"

"Of course you should. I want to work on myself too."

I didn't need telling twice, "You let your rabbi think for you. Why can't you decide for yourself?"

He sighed, "I *have* decided. I *choose* to ask him and I *trust* his judgment. What do you think? That I'm smarter than him? That *you're* smarter than him?" He sighed again, "look, let's not focus on that now. I've always accepted you for who you are and I think we both have where to grow. I really think we could both compromise and make this work."

Nesanel was right. Every relationship requires compromises, giving and taking and growing together. On one hand, he was so frustrating, on the other hand, he was so smart and understanding, handsome and sweet. And it would only get better, once we're engaged, married, once we'd go on real dates.

Was I exaggerating? What was he asking me to do? Spend an hour a week in a *shiur*? He was right, I did want to grow.

I found a *shiur* on Jewish philosophy in my neighborhood and got excited. I told Nesanel about it and he said that his rabbi had something else in mind. The rabbi suggested a trusty rebbetzin an hour away and I sat through her boring *tznius halacha* classes.

We met each other's parents.

"My rabbi said your mother's second earring is okay because she's Israeli and it means something different culturally... but she should take it out by the wedding."

At the wedding, the three of us stood under the chuppah: Nesanel, his rabbi and me.

We got married and he told me he really loved me and finally was able to tell me I'm beautiful and hold my hand. But only in private, his rabbi said, it's not *tznius* otherwise.

False Name, True Love

I friended Rena because we had four mutual friends, also because she looked a bit familiar, her thick hair and narrow waist, must have seen her around the neighborhood? Met her at a party? Maybe her parents knew my parents, maybe I knew her cousins?

Who am I kidding, she didn't look familiar one bit. She looked super-hot and I sent the friend request before thinking twice.

The notification from Messenger still surprised me:

'*Do you always friend random girls or just me?*'

I grinned at my phone and typed back, '*I try not to make a habit of it.*'

Typing...typing...she liked to use suspense, had me wait ten full minutes: '*Wow, I feel honored.*'

'*I'm surprised we haven't met before, it seems all our friends know each other.*' I wrote.

'*I have a lot of friends.*'

I checked her profile real quick. She wasn't exaggerating, over a thousand friends. Popular girl. I wondered what she made of my meager four-hundred. Well, I make a point of only friending people I actually know... until now.

I asked her why she has so many friends.

She asked me why I'm so anti-social.

I told her I wasn't, I just like a real connection.

She said, '*I can tell.*' Was that sarcasm?

'*What about you?*' I asked.

'*I like shallow conversations and fake relationships,*' she typed back. Yep, definitely sarcastic.

So I kept the conversation shallow, '*who took your profile picture?*' The photo was professional, dramatic, in front of a sunset.

'*A friend,*' she wrote, and then, '*you like it?*'

'*It's okay,*' I lied. The camera caught the moment her serious expression cracked into a smile. It was both mysterious and unguarded, '*I've seen better.*'

She typed and paused, typed and sent nothing. A few minutes later she went offline. I stayed on for another look at her (perfect) profile picture and then went off as well. I wondered if I messed this up if I acted too mean.

Whatever. I moved on, took a shower, made a sandwich, read the internet—

But then I saw the notification from Rena and my stomach leaped. Leaped double when I saw what she'd written:

'*Yours isn't too bad.*'

And that's the story of how my relationship with the beautiful stranger, Rena Sweet began (I highly suspected the last name was a fake but it suited her).

It began slowly. She'd disappear for an hour, I'd also disappear—for two or three hours, ha! Just to play it cool, to show her how little I cared.

But then I cared, and so did she, desperately, cared. Our texting became relentless, non-stop. From the moment I woke up—'*what's your day look like?*' Until I was back to bed at night, '*... thinking of you.*'

I learned so much about her, from the way she liked to wear her hair to the fight she had with her mother.

'It's about my skirts,' she wrote, 'I wish she would just leave me alone and let me do whatever the hell I want.'

I didn't know much about skirt arguments with mothers, or any sort of argument with parents over stuff like that, my parents are super open-minded and accepting. They're religious, but didn't mind when I stopped wearing a *kippa*. *It's between you and God*, they said.

But I did know—from what I saw through the pictures she posted, and she posted a *lot*: 'I like your skirts. I think they make your legs look hot.'

She sent a mirror selfie in a skirt shorter than the ones she posted online. I liked it even more.

She knew everything there was to know about me, that my favorite food was burgers, that I watched Friends five times—she'd never even watched it!—that I played basketball, and worked out and recently finished my service in the IDF and I felt free and liberated and accomplished and... utterly lost.

'My parents say that the army is bad,' she wrote.

'Don't believe them.' I typed back.

We texted back and forth for a week. And then I called, listening to her hushed whisper on the other end of the line. Once a day in the evening. I lived for those phone calls. The sound of her voice said more than her typed words could, like the way she paused between certain words. It made her thoughtful and deliberate. I imagined her sprawled on her bed, curling her fingers through her hair. What was she wearing? Her nightgown? She sent me a picture when I asked.

It was too much. This tease. Beautiful Rena, did she realize how deep in I was? Did she realize I was falling in love?

It was stupid, obsessive even, the way I was acting, but— as cliché as it sounds—she's the first girl that's made me feel this way in a while. That made me feel like I wanted more than just a hookup.

'I want to see you.' I told her on Sunday, held my breath and by Thursday she agreed.

We met in a park, twenty minutes away from my house in Modi'in, she came all the way by bus from Beit Shemesh. I told her I'd pick her up and we'd go to a restaurant at any bright and cozy mall near her but she said this was better.

I sat on a bench in a light jacket—it was early spring— and searched the distance for long legs. She'd wear her hair down over one shoulder, I guessed, and the flats she bought last week. She sent me a picture of them, but I told her it's only interesting if she's wearing it.

"Hi."

I jumped a mile and caught my breath, "Rena?"

She sat next to me, how had she gotten here? It was her though, my Rena, serious face breaking into a smile. We hugged, and I was wrong, her hair was up in a pony. I took it out and pulled it over her shoulder just as she liked it.

"Rena!" I said again.

How had I missed her? I looked down, her legs were buried in black fabric, a long skirt that reached her flats.

Her skirt... I pinched at the fabric that spilled onto the bench, thick and stretchy.

"I thought you'd wear the other one." I winked and laughed.

She looked taken aback, "I'd never wear *that* outside."

We sat on the bench and stayed like that for a long time. She leaned on my chest and stared at the stars, I stared at her eyes and we spoke.

"How was your day?"

"How was *yours?*"

"Did you miss me?"

"How could I miss someone I don't know?"

"I missed you. I feel like I know you."

"I've never touched a boy before."

"Should I stop?" I didn't want to stop running my hand through her hair.

"No, it's nice."

I paused and stared deeper into her eyes, she stared straight back. There was a moment and her eyes fluttered closed, her body went stiff on my lap. Nervous, she was excited but terrified, I felt it.

I took a deep breath and looked away, better to take things slow. Better not to scare her.

We met up the following Sunday, again in the park.

"It's a miracle I found you," I told her and took her hair down again.

"You believe in miracles?"

"I believe in *you*," we kissed gently. We made out all night, on the grass in the park. It was damp but we didn't care.

At the bus stop, she told me she doesn't know when she could see me again.

"Tomorrow," I told her. Plain and simple. Texting wouldn't do anymore, not even phone calls would do.

We met up on Monday, in a different park with more jackets for the cold. Just meant more layers to shed when it got hot.

We went out on Tuesday.

"You're right. It is a miracle." She finally agreed, "Just last month I opened Facebook, and now I'm here with you."

We went out on Wednesday. I came to Beit Shemesh this time even though she told me not to. She had me wait in the darkest park for her.

Thursday—I saw her every day of the week so far and couldn't imagine it any other way.

"I can't do this anymore, I want to take you out properly, to a restaurant. I'll drive you home after, please let me."

Rena shook her head, "I don't want people to see us."

"Why not?"

"It's not good for *shidduchim*," she sighed and rolled her eyes, "I'm starting to date soon… reputation and all that," she laughed it off.

I wasn't laughing.

"Aren't we… going out now?"

"Going out like dating?"

I nodded.

"No," she looked at me funny, "you're not religious."

"Oh," I didn't know what else to say, "um… okay."

The Pessimist and the Dreamer

Chaim and I were getting pretty serious. We'd gone out for nearly a full month and my mother was sick with the stress that he hadn't proposed yet.

"It's me," I told her, "I'm not ready yet. I want to wait a little longer."

"Chaim will see you're not committed," my mother warned me, "oy, he could find someone else and get engaged by the time you 'feel ready.'"

She was right, it was risky and with each passing day some of her stress rubbed off on me. It wasn't even that I wasn't ready, I really was. I was eighteen years old and as ready as I'd ever been... but I still hadn't discussed it with him. I wasn't even sure how to broach the topic so instead, I avoided it. We'd go out for lunch and we'd speak about schools again, the types we'd like to send our kids to. We'd speak about hashkafa again, the most important mitzvos for a man and woman to keep—I'd be the Zevulan to his Yisaschar, and bring that Torah into our home. We'd discussed parsha and events, styles and ideas. We'd discuss topics we'd already discussed and our conversation turned boring. This is why couples don't go out for too long—the magic dies once there's nothing more to say. With engagement comes planning, the sparks of nerves and excitement, and then you have kids and the magic fully returns. I wanted that.

I was stalling.

I wasn't talking about the one thing I wanted to talk about.

"I think we should get engaged sooner than later," Chaim said. We were out in a restaurant waiting for our order to arrive.

"Of course," I said.

"You don't look so sure..."

"It's not that."

"What is it?"

I planned what to say but it came out in a jumble: "I wanted to bring it up before we get engaged. It's not my idea, don't worry. My cousin was telling me about it and said it was important and I should bring it up when I'm dating. I don't usually bring things like this up, you know that but she was telling me stories—not that chas v'shalom they apply to us, but it's for the community she was saying—"

"What are you talking about?"

"What? Oh. Yeah. I didn't say. I think we should sign the halachic prenup. Like once we're engaged of course." I smiled and fidgeted with the hem of my shirt.

A beat passed. Chaim took a deep breath, leaned in his seat and said, "Are we really talking about this now?"

"What do you mean?"

"I am talking about engagement," he paused, "and you are talking about divorce. I just want to make sure that we're going in the same direction..."

"Of course we're going in the same direction. And I am looking forward," I stammered, "I'm not even talking about divorce, of course not," I laughed lightly, "I'm talking about signing a piece of paper."

"Yeah, going through all the hassle to sign another paper we'll just put away. I get it! You're worried we don't have what to do," he gave an ironic laugh, "once we're in wedding preparations we'll have enough on our plate. Trust me."

"I'm not bored," I snapped, surprised at my assertiveness but also proud. There is nothing wrong with talking about the prenup, I added, "and who said we can't talk about divorce?"

Chaim pressed his hands into his eyes and rubbed his face and began, "Look, I don't know what you're taught in your home, but in mine, we're taught that marriage is marriage—through thick and thin. Through all the problems. You work through them and make it work. Hmm," he tapped his chin as he thought, "that's what you see on the TV, right—all the stars getting divorced after a year? If they get married at all. I'm sorry I just don't have that goyish mindset."

"I'm not saying I want to get divorced. Chas v'shalom!" I nearly sobbed, "My cousin was just telling me how it's important to sign so that it becomes a standard… so no woman is stuck in a marriage."

"So this is feminist talk?" Chaim shook his head, "I should've known. All these pessimistic women thinking the worst of men. Please don't tell me you're like that too. Please don't tell me."

A waiter came with our order and we went silent. He placed it in front of us and Chaim thanked him politely. I looked around the restaurant, suddenly aware that we were in a very public place and people could have overheard our awkward conversation. Baruch Hashem, I didn't see any neighbors or family friends around. If word got back to my mother...

"I... you're right. Of course. I just thought it was a nice idea," I forced myself to laugh.

Chaim didn't understand this stuff, I realized. He was just too good, he can't even imagine a situation where someone would withhold a Get so he just sees my request as absurd. Well, it's a nice idea for couples that need it, at least we're not in that situation, "you're right, it's quite ridiculous for me to bring it up."

"Now we can talk about engagement?"

"And marriage," I smiled.

"Through thick and thin?"

"Forever." I agreed.

Quite the Catch

I'm quite the catch, I'm not saying this to show off. Ask all my friends, they'll tell you I'm the least *gaayvadik* guy they know. *But* I am close to the top of my shiur, quite handsome and even tall—nearly five foot ten! Also, my grandparents have apartments in Rechavia and accounts for each of my six siblings awaiting us on our wedding day.

I'm also awaiting my wedding day, quite impatiently at this point. My rabbi sat me down last month and told me, "Do you think you're ready for *shidduchim*?"

"Not yet," I said, but the rest of the day I couldn't think of anything else. A *shidduch*? Sounds intense, but then I thought a bit more. What is a *shidduch*? Some awesome, perfect girl that's mine forever, that I could do whatever I want with. We could live for some years in those apartments in Rechavia, my grandparents would trust me just because I'm married (unlike last year when I asked to move in). *Everyone* would trust me once I'm married. Marriage was that level-up in society, wasn't it?

I'm an old fashioned guy, I'd also find a wife that would make me food and iron my shirts. I could be modern too, I'd let her work if she wanted, but nothing more than part-time. I wouldn't want my wife to work too hard. The idea just sounded better and better.

I just got off the phone with my mother. She told me about the newest prospect: "Chana's a darling girl. The references only had good things to say. She's in seminary, getting a degree in physiology at the same time. Her father's a doctor so they must have money. Did you see her picture? She's really pretty too."

"I couldn't tell... does she have long hair?"

"Sixteen inches," she said, "I think that length is great because it shows she's *tznius* but still cares about looking good."

I wasn't sure how sixteen inches looked but my mother knew her stuff.

Oh, *shidduchim*. Last time this year I couldn't have imagined myself in this position. Well, I couldn't have imagined myself anywhere really. That's how lost I was. That's actually why I came to Israel in the first place. *Hashgacha pratis* if you will.

I wanted to get away. I wanted uncensored internet and I wanted to talk to girls, so I said to my parents, "I really want to learn in a serious environment. All the messed up kids are staying behind. I know what's going to happen to them and I don't want that happening to me. Besides, isn't everything more spiritual in Israel?"

It's been years up to that point that I'd picked up a *sefer* with any ounce of seriousness so my parents smiled at me with their hopes and dreams shining in their eyes and shipped me off to Israel.

It was a year of experiences. Of wearing tight jeans and going to bars.

"I can't take the cornflakes here, it tastes like cardboard, it tastes like nothing!" I complained to my mother on the phone. She added a hundred shekel to my weekly budget. I suffered through cardboard and milk all week, spending the

Fruity Pebbles fund on Thursday night beer. A liter cost about the same much as a box.

I had my first kiss in the back of Mike's Place. I knew she'd let because she wore jeans tighter than mine.

"How old are you?" I asked her after downing the equivalent cost of a month of American cereal in beer.

"Twenty," she lied, "you?"

"Twenty-one," I lied too. I could tell she lied because I recognized her from Facebook, we had mutual friends and she was eighteen like me.

"I got you a drink," I said and slid into the booth next to her. I was nervous so I drank more.

She checked me out and made up her mind, waving at her friends across the bar that it was fine.

I checked her out too, hard not to with her glaringly opened t-shirt. She cut the neckline so that it slipped off her shoulders. Her bra straps were hot pink. I've never seen so much of a bra before.

Shira and I met up a few times after that. I got to see a lot more things I hadn't seen before. I liked spending time with her.

A month or two later we met up and her eyes were red, "I'm going home."

"Oh, that's fine." I said. I knew girls can get emotional, I could be patient with that, "we can meet up another night."

"No, I'm going home. *Home*, home." she repeated, "they found out, I'm flying back to New York."

Found out about what? I wondered.

"They found out about *us*," she whispered, "we'll keep in touch, won't we?"

I nodded, hugged her tight and inhaled her strawberry smelling hair. Then I kissed her good-bye and went as far as she'd let me—not very far, sad girls weren't as fun. The next Thursday night in town I wondered if it was as easy finding someone else. It took some time and insistence but Noa was game. She had an awesome body and was way more experimental than Shira.

After Noa there was Gila and Mina, they were both cute and fun so I'd meet up with them on different nights.

Everything changed towards the end of the year. After Pesach, when the weather got warm. There was a party in Tel Aviv of a friend of a friend's friend. I'd been to parties in Tel Aviv before and they were all wild. I wore my tightest jeans and no yarmulke.

What I remember of the night:

I was quiet but eventually warmed up to the people I barely knew. The girls wore less clothing here. Everyone was taking something. I took it too.

In the morning my head ached, my shirt was stained, my arm was bruised and I remembered none of it. Gigi thanked me for coming to her party, she said I'm welcome any time.

I threw up, put my shirt on, and ran to the bus straight to Yerushalayim.

A few days later a friend said, "You know Lily? She's having a birthday party tomorrow night, all her friends will be there. She insisted I invite my friend 'Steve'." He rolled his eyes.

All my friends knew I liked to call myself Steve when I went out and went along with it even though they thought it was ridiculous.

"You go without me," I said, "I'm not feeling well."

Thursday night didn't carry the same excitement it always did, it even elicited a sort of dread. The dread of peeing in alleys and splitting headaches in the morning. Of loud music, of chilled music, of the taste and smell of cigarettes on everyone's tongue. Of feeling drunk or high or both. And mostly of feeling empty.

I found myself in the *makolet* choosing out cereals for the week instead. I found myself rethinking my motives in

Israel, recalculating what really matters. Thinking if I want these instant relationships and nights I can barely remember, clouded with drugs and alcohol or if I want something more... something pure.

And I realized, I should have ended this with Shira, I realized, I should have ended this before Shira—before it all started.

So I woke up for Shachris, I let my friends down. I made new friends, one that actually showed up to seder. I grew. The rabbis smiled at me, told me they were proud. My mother heard the difference in my tone on the phone, told me she was proud.

Two weeks home in the summer and then I was back, for another year. This time to do it right. This wasn't what I came to Israel for but it's what I found anyways, everything is more spiritual here, after all, right? Like I said, *hashgacha pratis.*

Finally, I was ready for a good girl to build a good home with. I was ready to be the best husband I could be for her.

"So what do you say?" my mother asked over speakerphone.

"What's her name again?"

"Chana Goldberg."

I quickly typed her name in the Facebook search bar. I still had my smartphone, I couldn't give it up and with the help of an internet filter I was keeping things kosher. The fifth Chana Goldberg on the list looked like the one. I clicked on her profile and did a quick run through. It was mostly sparse—a private account, some modesty, that's good, I recently put my account on private too.

I clicked on her profile picture. It was a photo from a wedding and Chana looked great, hair done up and a sparkly pink gown. I went through the photos, liking what I saw. Chana, last year in a knit sweater in a field. Younger Chana, smiling with a friend. Chana in hiking gear—a black skirt and long leggings—waving from the top of Masada. Chana at a summer camp—I paused.

The photo was Chana in summer camp, the sun glistening off of her arms, *bare* arms, with sleeves only covering a few inches down her shoulders. I clicked next and there was another one. Chana in short sleeves, this time with an open neck too. The photo was from 2014, not even too long ago. I took a deep breath and tried to judge favorably. It was a hard *middah* to work on.

The next picture and her skirt hit above her knees. It reminded me of the girls in town that just wanted attention, any attention they could get.

"You knew she wasn't religious once?" I asked my mother, clicking on yet *another* photo with her arms on display to the world.

"I think she was brought up more modern," my mother explained, "she's in a great seminary now."

"Ma!" I groaned, "You know I don't want a girl with a past."

"Oh," my mother frowned, "those things really mess young girls up, don't they?"

She told the *shadchan* it wasn't *shayach*. The *shadchan* called back and said, "Well, I have another girl to offer. Her name is Yael and..."

Love at First Sights

Love at first sight. I didn't believe in the concept—until I met Esti, that is. From the moment I laid eyes on her in the grand doorway to her four-story mansion, I felt it, the swell in my heart. She knew just what to say, broke the ice immediately as she got into the car, telling me about her brother's bar mitzvah last week on a charter yacht.

"That sounds amazing," I said, imagining our own wedding in a castle-like hall with the best meat and imported spirits.

"But I enjoyed the Shabbos more than the party," she said, "its nice spending time in the hotel with my extended family."

That's how our *Shabbos sheva brachos* would be, I decided, a five-star hotel, so we can truly get to know each other's families properly.

I was good looking, charming and sweet but I knew I needed an extra something to win her love so I brought her to the most expensive restaurant I knew—the smartest investment I could make in my future.

We had a fabulous time, and when the waiter charged two hundred dollars on my card I barely flinched.

Before I dropped her off, we smiled goofily at each other for a full minute straight. It was the love in the air, it was infectious and she felt it too.

"Cancel the date with Tehilla," I told my mother first thing, "I'm going out with Esti again."

And again, and again, and again and again. Until our wedding in the castle and our honeymoon to Hawaii...or maybe Africa? I've always wanted to visit the safari.

"You know I can't do that," my mother said, "you have to go out with Tehilla at least once, you'll embarrass us if not. And her! Think of how she will feel if you cancel so suddenly.

And if the *shadchan* finds out..." she continued to herself, shaking her head and thinking the worst.

The date with Tehilla was a huge mistake. I agreed to go out with her with one *shadchan* without knowing that my mother already told another *shadchan* that I was available to date Esti. Two dates, I was only one man.

"Just take her out for an hour," she said again, "we'll tell the *shadchan* you tried and that's it. You'll continue with Esti."

The following night, I barely brushed my hair, showed up late to Tehilla's door. It was small and plain compared to Esti's grand entranceway.

Tehilla opened the door and I stopped dead in my tracks.

She was gorgeous. Hands down the hottest women I'd ever seen. Flawless smile and curves even her modest dress couldn't hide. Love at first sight. My jaw dropped and for a moment I couldn't react.

I blew another two hundred bucks in the same fancy restaurant begging the waiters with my eyes not to show signs of recognition. The best investment I could make.

It bought me three hours in close proximity to Tehilla.

She was charming and sweet and easy to talk to and easy to look at—easy to stare at. I had to stop myself more than once to focus on the actual words she was saying. The way her lips formed words. Entrancing. Hypnotizing. Seductive.

I tried to ooh and ah in the right places.

"Thanks for tonight," Tehilla said back at her house, "I really had a nice time."

Her smile made my heart stop and all I could do was nod.

"Was that so hard?" my mother said at home, "Now you never have to see that girl again."

I froze, my brain on a frenzy of rejection. No, no, no, no, no. I wanted to see Tehilla again. I *needed* to. I was in love after all.

But I already scheduled a date with Esti tomorrow night. I groaned and buried my face in my hands, took a deep breath and pulled myself together. One more date with Esti, than I could drop her and move onto Tehilla, my one true love.

"Keep it short," my mother warned, "you don't want to lead her on."

I pulled up in front of Esti's mansion and walked up the path to her front door. It was lined with fancy flowers and bushes preened to perfection.

Esti opened the door in a sparkly dress with diamonds studding her ears. God, I forgot how much I loved this woman.

My palms grew sweaty, I hadn't planned anything extravagant. But I wanted her to love me back. Please, Hashem, let her love me.

"It's okay," Esti sensed my nerves and reassured as we walked to the car, "I'm a simple girl. Anywhere you take me is good."

We went to my favorite restaurant, not nearly as expensive as the first but the burgers were great and came with extra meat. It was a risky move, I knew, but I had to put her to the test. I was nearly sold by the dress and jewelry but if she didn't like these burgers she wasn't for me, I'm sure Tehilla would love them.

She bit into her giant burger, sauce exploding on her cheeks, and laughed as she wiped them clean.

"This is really good!"

"Right?" I grinned.

Burgers and designer dresses. They matched horribly and perfectly and Esti worked them both so well.

We laughed and ate and spoke about our hobbies. I loved relaxing, she loved shopping. We both loved looking at beautiful things.

Tehilla was beautiful.

I picked her up the following night and was completely right about her. She loved the burgers.

"I come here all the time with my friends," she said and looked like the poster girl for burgers as she took her first bite. I wanted to snap a picture and keep it forever, better yet, keep her forever.

We were out until the restaurant closed. She enjoyed, I enjoyed. This was going somewhere good.

"Yaakov had two wives," I announced at home, "why don't Jews do that today. I want to be like our *Avos*."

My mother wasn't having any of it, "choose a girl or I'm going to call them both off!"

"No!"

It really wasn't fair. I was sure I could handle it, two wives. Why did society ever call off such a beautiful concept? Esti and Tehilla. I could share my love equally, just like I was now.

Regardless I took a breath and wrote the lists. Pros and cons. It was hard when both had a collection of pros and no cons to counter

They were both pretty, both fashionable, both kind and sweet, with good *middos* and great mindsets. So Tehilla had more in the looks and Esti had more in the fashion. So what? They'd both make great wives and excellent mothers.

Oh Hashem, I wondered, what I did to deserve this *nisayon*? After countless dates that led nowhere with stupid girls or ugly girls or poor girls or all three, why, oh why did I get sent these two gems at once?

I went out with Esti and I knew it was the last time, I'd have to call it off. Money comes and goes, looks stay forever.

But Esti looked beautiful tonight. Her hair was up and the gold chain on her delicate neck sparkled. We played glow in the dark mini golf and she smiled the whole time.

Tehilla enjoyed too. She said she's never played mini golf in the dark before and the dim lighting made her glow even more.

"I feel like this is really going somewhere," I told them both after our dates.

They agreed.

"You're not going out with both of them again," my mother said, "I don't let. You have to choose one."

It was the choice of my life, literally. I was choosing my companion, my life partner, the woman I'd share children with. The woman I'd build a home with.

Esti was so spiritual, she said '*baruch Hashem*' all the time. Tehilla was so motherly, I could tell by the way she

130

spoke about her little siblings. Esti really knew how to enjoy life. Tehilla really knew how to make the best of little moments.

I went to sleep thinking of both of them with terrible longing. There was one I thought of more.

I announced my decision in the morning, I'd take care of it quickly, no regrets. My mother said I should call her directly, I've been out with her enough, it's only fair.

The phone rang twice and she picked up.

My heart hurt before I even spoke.

"Hi, listen, I've been thinking about it for a long time…You're really amazing, I just don't think it's going to work out between us."

She was terribly hurt, wished me good luck, that Hashem should help me find my match soon. No worries there.

As I said, Esti was super spiritual. I knew she'd find someone perfect for her soon. She really deserved the best.

It's better this way, I told myself, now I can fully focus all my energy on my one true love, the sooner we go out, the better. I really wanted to see her soon.

The more I thought about it, the surer I felt. A weight off my shoulders because I could completely and entirely give my heart to Tehilla. I'd treat her like a queen when I saw her,

I'd spend all my money on her. She deserved it all. She deserved the best.

Later in the day my mother smiled grimly and told me the news. Tehilla told the *shadchan*, "I don't think he's for me. Something about the connection. I feel like he's not fully there."

Curiosity Killed the Cat

I met him at the ice skating rink, *Motzei Shabbos.* He was cute and well dressed, in a local yeshiva and nineteen years old. I was eighteen and girlishly stupid and fell for him immediately. The whole time while skating we had our eyes on each other. At first, we pretended to be discreet but then we outright stared.

After the hour, I pulled my skates off on the bench, carefully checking for new blisters.

"I have to pee," my friend said.

I took my time, "just go, I'll catch up."

She left and *he* popped up.

"You're from around here?" He asked and casually tied his shoes on the bench beside me. His shoes looked so big next to mine.

"Yeah, you?"

"Yep."

"It's a wonder I never see you around."

"I'd like to see you around more," he said and smiled.

I agreed, gave over my number and left in a daze to find my friend.

His name was Yoni and he messaged me that night.

We didn't have much to say, small talk about ice skating, common friends we might have, where we lived and went to school and then Yoni said, "Let's meet up."

We met for Slurpees even though I hated them. He drank half of his before we tossed them out and went back to his car.

We spoke for a bit, it seemed the only thing we had in common was *Motzei Shabbos* ice skating. He told me about his stupid friends, how they came over for Xbox battles until dawn, I wished him good luck and wondered why he wasted his time. I told him about Yoko from the nail salon, she did the best job but recently she hasn't been around. I basically felt Yoni's eye roll.

He was really cute, with manly eyebrows and big shoulders, and I could tell where this was leading to, alone in his car and he insisted we sit in the backseat, so I waited for it to happen, curious and patient. I answered questions that I didn't care about and asked back shortly, until we didn't have to keep that up.

It happened in stages. Slow at the time but indiscernible in memory. First, he held my hands, then pulled me close. I got to see his out-of-hand-eyebrows up close, got to feel his prickly cheek brushing against mine. Then we kissed and it was nice.

We met up a lot after that, at night in Yoni's parent's car, skipping the unbearable talking part that neither of us enjoyed and jumping right into it. It was more fun that way and honestly what we both wanted.

We met up nearly every night and sometimes in the day, when he'd get off Yeshiva and I'd stay home from school, we'd refrain from holding hands all down Avenue J, but the second we got on the subway, we couldn't keep apart. He'd squeeze my shoulder, I'd hold his hand. Our relationship was a hundred percent physical and we both preferred it this way.

Central Park was the best. Broad daylight, cuddling on the grass and no one batted an eye. We were socially invisible with the thrill of public visibility.

We were getting too confident, too risky, feeling too young and invincible, making out in local driveways. I shouldn't be surprised at the way it ended.

He snuck me into his house. It was like a game of cops and robbers, ridiculous and refreshing and when I made it through his side door, up two flights of steps and home-free in his bedroom I laughed hysterically with a hand over my mouth to shut myself up. As if anyone was home. Eleven on a weekday morning and we had the whole day with no one around. His mother comes home at two, I had to disappear before that. Until then I could walk around any way I liked. We could do whatever we want.

The hours blurred.

Two o'clock came and went and we barely noticed.

Four o'clock and his little siblings came home. We heard them run through the doors and up the stairs, their voices outside his room.

"You have to stay here until nine. That's when Gila and Aaron go to sleep. Then we could sneak you out." Yoni whispered. We turned the lights off and hid under the blankets just for fun.

"What if I have to go to the bathroom?"

"You'll pee in a bottle and we'll throw it out the window."

As I said it I realized I had to pee badly. I held it in.

"My parents!" I remembered, "I have to tell them something. They'll freak out."

I called my mom and said, "I'm by Chani...oh, I didn't tell you I was studying with her for the Chumash test?"

"We have so much more to study!" Yoni said in the weirdest high pitched tone, imitating 'Chani.' I squeezed his arm to shut him up, trying not to laugh, I said to my mom, "yep. Lots to study. I'll be home after nine."

"C'mon, let's study!" Yoni said in his best Chani voice and I hung up before I burst out laughing on the phone.

Our stomachs rumbled together

"What about food?" I asked.

"Should I go downstairs and bring something up?"

"Will your family be suspicious?"

He didn't risk it. Instead, we chewed gum because that's the only thing I had in my purse and waited. The need to pee passed. His hand was on my stomach and I played with his fingers—

"Stop!" I yelped.

"What?" he said and did it again.

He tickled me!

"Don't—do—that," I said through pants of laughter—

The door handle creaked. We clutched each other in nerves. Someone tried it! It was locked though. They knocked and banged.

"Yoni, open the door."

"Not now," Yoni called back and I squeezed him so tight, my nails left marks in his forearm, "I'm busy."

"Open up right now."

"Please, Ma—I'm...I'm in the middle of Tehillim."

She didn't answer. We stayed still for what felt like a year and finally her footsteps faded down the hall.

"Oh no," I bit my lip, "you think she heard me? Are we in trouble?"

"It's okay," Yoni assured me and stood up. His shirt was unbuttoned and rumpled. Mine was even worse. I fixed it as best as I could.

We waited through the last agonizing hour in silence until nine and then a little more time just to be safe.

I fled out the side door before anyone saw me.

I thought that would be the end of it. Yoni didn't even text me and I was scared to text him too. It was better this way, to pretend it never happened, even though my body missed him in a way I never knew it could. Whatever. He was a stupid guy anyways with nothing ever intelligent to say. I'd get married really soon to someone double as smart and just as good in *that* field.

Of course, it wasn't the end of it. Of course not. When were things ever so simple? Two days later, my mother sat me down.

"I spoke to Feinsteins about you and their son."

I waited.

"We also spoke to Mrs. Lebovitch from the bakery and Gitty Weiss from down the block."

"Okay..."

"They're all saying the same thing."

"Hmm," I looked away.

"Other neighbors too," my mother shook her head, "I don't get it, don't you care?"

"Care about what?"

"About your future."

I shrugged, "I like Yoni."

"Good! He's the best you're going to get at this point," my mother burst.

I opened my mouth to protest but my mother cut me off again, loud and angry—

"You thought no one would notice? What do you think this is? This is our neighborhood that you're part of and now your name is written in black ink. You want to get set up with a good guy now? Ha!"

Yoni is a good guy, I wanted to say but didn't.

"Why are you so angry at me?"

"You are such a selfish little girl," my mother scolded, "you think this is all about you. You don't realize you're embarrassing the whole family. Did you think of how hard it is for Tatty to show his face in Shul? For Ariella, you're already ruining her prospects."

Ariella was in tenth grade and the perfect, golden child. She always wore a skirt two inches longer than it had to be and never spoke to a boy in her life. I wasn't worried about her.

But suddenly I was. Could it really affect her? What I did with Yoni in his car down our block, those hours of making out... was it worth it?

"What should I do?" I groaned.

"What choice do you have?"

"What do you mean?"

"You're going to get engaged to that boy," my mother said, "His parents agree."

"It's not their place to agree," I said hotly, "it's mine and Yoni's" and no way I'm gonna settle for a loser like him, I didn't say.

"What choices do you think you have? You think anyone's going to want you? It's a miracle they even agreed to let Yoni have you, well, seeing you both can't keep your hands to yourselves..."

I texted Yoni that night.

"Did your parents speak to you?" I wrote.

"Yeah, yours?"

Duh. That's why I'm asking. He was so dense.

"What do you think?"

"Once we're engaged, you think they'll let us get it on?"

I threw the phone aside and cuddled alone in bed.

Entering Shabbos, I announced to my parents, "I won't marry him." My father looked down and my mother took a deep breath. I planned on ignoring them but they didn't even notice—because they were already ignoring me. The whole night they didn't address me once.

"Ariella, how was your week?"

"Chaim Dovid, do you have a *dvar Torah* to share?"

"Mindy, what do they teach about the *parsha* in kindergarten?"

"Ta, can you pass the challah?" I asked. He still kept his eyes off me, "Tatty?"

It was too much, too unbearable. By the time Sunday came around, I *had* to get out.

I called Chani, "let's go to the mall."

"Look," she said in a tone I'd never heard her use before, "look," she repeated, "I know it shouldn't matter and I'm not judging you…"

"What?" it came out aggressive. I didn't mean for it to.

"I'm sorry. I can't just hang around with girls that shtup random guys… people will think I'm like that too. You get me, right? You know I love you."

Of course. Of course, I totally understand. I hung up and hated Chani's guts.

Would they let us get it on once we're engaged? I wondered to myself as I cuddled with a blanket at night and checked my phone for no new messages, from no friend that wanted to risk their reputation on me.

No, it turned out, they didn't let. Every time Yoni was by me or I was by him we'd have to leave the door opened. They never either let us take the car privately, as if that stopped us.

If they're making me marry this guy, I figured, I'd better enjoy him in the only way I can.

Hock on the Block

"So, you're not going out with that girl anymore?" Yehuda asked. It was Friday night and I was at his house. We usually got together for an oneg Shabbos, us and a couple of guys. Tonight, it was just us. We cracked opened beers, brought out the chips and filled each other in on the hock.

"Who, Shani?" I said, "I broke it off a few weeks ago."

"Oh," Yehuda frowned, "I thought it was going so well."

"It was…" I paused and remembered our dates. Shani was a great girl. We hit it off on the first date, staying out hours more than was appropriate. My mother scolded me. I didn't care. Every date after only got better. I could talk to her about anything, everything, from Kim Kardashian to Parshas Lech Lecha. She wasn't a fan of the Kardashian butt, although she liked their fashion line, she was inspired by Avraham's courage and hoped one day she could have that same courage too.

"So you want to move to Eretz Yisroel?" I had asked her.

"Wherever Hashem leads me," she had said and I knew that she'd really meant, "Wherever my husband takes me." Perfect wife material.

This was all besides for her being drop dead gorgeous. Shani had big eyes and red lips, long hair and a butt to challenge any Kardashian. Even though she wasn't a fan, I sure was. "Did I show you her picture?"

Yoni shook his head.

"I'll have to show it to you sometime," I still had it on my phone, sometimes at night I'd look at it and smile and wonder 'what if.' What if engagement? What if marriage? What if that hot girl with the nice butt was mine? But then I'd close the picture and let it go. There were other fish in the sea and Monsey was a vast sea indeed. There were girls left and right: single, gorgeous, and hopelessly desperate. My mother had an endless waiting list of resumes to get through. I'd find The One by Rosh Hashana, she promised.

"So what happened?" Yehuda asked, "Why'd you end it?"

"My mom did some digging…"

"Yeah?"

"Well, she didn't have to dig so deep." I paused, "Look, I knew something was up with Shani's parents before she ever said anything."

"Yeah?" Yehuda pressed.

"So they're married for fifteen years, yeah?"

"Yeah."

"Seven kids—Shani's the third. Now, from the outside, it all looks perfect, as any one of the houses on this block. Nice, frum, home. And then—surprise, surprise, one day, a few months ago, the mom picks up and leaves. Next thing you know, they're divorced."

"No."

"Yeah. No one suspected a thing. Anyways when I ask Shani about it, she says it's nothing major. 'They fell out of love'. The family didn't want to make a big deal out of it, chas v'shalom the kids will get kicked out of school, the neighbors will talk," I shook my head at the absurdity of a family keeping such a big secret, "the mom had enough I guess. She totally left him."

I shook my head, "can you believe it? Full on divorce."

"That's crazy." Yehuda agreed.

Ridiculous

She was in class with me at Bar Ilan. I noticed her on the first
day. She was an *oleh chadash* like me and looked exactly like
Bar Rafaeli. That's not what caught my eye though, it was her
energy. The way she spoke that got everyone listening, the
way she laughed that got everyone laughing. She was
religious too—she wore a skirt and a cardigan.

Every time I looked back she was smiling or laughing or
deep in conversation with someone new. It seemed like

everyone was vying for her attention. When the lecture began I could barely pay attention, hyper-focused on her whispers.

After class, I found her in the café on campus.

"Hey, is it okay if I sit here?" I gestured to the seat opposite her at the empty table.

"Sure."

"Great," I smiled and slid into the seat across from her.

There was so much about her I wanted to know. I asked all the questions I could to get a clearer picture of the mysterious blonde.

Her name was Ayala, and she moved on her own from Teaneck, New Jersey, two years ago. Since, her sister joined her and her little brother was coming next year, planning to draft as a lone soldier.

"In the beginning it was difficult but I knew it's what I really wanted. I was either able to give up and move back or fight through. So I chose to fight."

"How's your Hebrew?"

She laughed, "Well, I definitely understand way more than I speak. My father is Israeli so I was always used to hearing Hebrew."

She asked about me too. It wasn't as interesting but I told her anyways, "my family moved eight years ago. I finished high school here, army... now I'm here, studying communications in Bar Ilan"

We would have spoken more but we were ten minutes late to our next class. Ayala jumped up and shouldered her bag in a frenzy.

It was the first day and I should have also felt bad about slacking but it was for a good cause. We walked to class together.

Next break we sat outside—it happened automatically, no discussion. I sought her as I was leaving the classroom. Our eyes met and she gravitated towards me. We found a bench in the shade of a tree.

"I think I'm going to fail," she said.

"Don't say that!" I said, "It's just the first day."

"Exactly, and I'm lost already," she groaned.

"Okay," I shrugged, "so just... give up I guess. Right?"

She laughed, "Fine, I'll get a degree."

"I'll study with you for tests. I'll force the information on you. You'll have no choice but to pass."

That first day I asked Ayala out:

"Um, well, I don't really know you well enough..."

"That's the point," I said, "You'll get to know me."

"Yeah...but what if it doesn't work out? It will be awkward."

"Nah. Awkward doesn't exist," Besides, I didn't tell her, I had no intention of this not working out.

She said no. I asked her the next day. She said no again. I asked her one more time. She sighed and rolled her eyes and finally said, "it doesn't have to be a date, okay? We can hang out. Casual."

I picked her up and brought her to the least casual restaurant I knew. A fancy chef restaurant in Tel Aviv.

"I don't think I'm wearing the right shoes for this," she said as we went up in the glass elevator.

I noticed her shoes—worn out Blundstones. "They're perfect," I said.

A waitress seated us. Ayala looked around, impressed and I smiled to myself.

"I'll have a tea," she decided after a few minutes.

"Are you serious, that's all?"

"Everything is so ridiculously expensive," she said, "I'd generally split, but this is too much."

I waved a hand dismissively, "get whatever you want. Please."

Dinner was fantastic. I ordered extra sides because I knew Ayala wouldn't and we shared everything. It wasn't that I was rich, I just knew where it was worth putting my money. I watched Ayala take a bite of some mushroom dish and knew this was worth every overpriced shekel. Her blue eyes were alight with wonder and pleasure. I stuck my fork into a mushroom to try it too.

Roses. This girl needs roses. In class when she was concentrating and taking notes, I unzipped her bag and carefully placed inside a handful of roses.

When Ayala reached in to get a charger, she smiled up at me and rolled her eyes.

She scrawled a message on her notebook and passed it to me: *are you for real?*

Why not? I wrote back

I still don't know you well enough, she wrote back.

I snorted, *so you'll have to get to know me better.*

She had extra ulpan classes. I studied in the library and went to her classroom when I knew she'd finish.

"You waited here for me?"

"No. I happened to be here and realized you finish now."

"Stop!" Ayala said but laughed.

I wanted to take her out again. She didn't let, "it's awkward! You can't just take me out and spend a million shekel on me."

"Excuse me," I faked anger, "I'm not spending it on *you*. I always go to that restaurant, I just asked you to join."

"Sure you do."

"Will you go with me for shawarma?"

"Come over. I'll cook something for us."

Even better. I grinned.

Her apartment was a fifteen-minute walk from the university. We cut vegetables together until she dismissed me because I was taking up too much space. The steaming homemade dish was just as good as that restaurant, if not better.

"You are amazing."

"You too," she said and it may have been sarcastic but I smiled anyway.

In school, I slipped a letter into her notebook. She didn't react until lunch.

Ayala,

You say I'm too much. You want us casual and comfortable. I tried and tried to do it your way but I can't anymore. I want you to be the happiest in the world and I want to be the one that makes you feel that way. No matter how much it costs, no matter how hard I'll have to try. You are worth everything and so much more.

Please, Ayala. Just let me.

"I have never met anyone as ridiculous as you!"

Before I let myself become crestfallen, I asked, "In a good way or a bad way?"

She sighed, "In the best way."

And I was giddy again, like a little kid that won a raffle.

"Where can we go to celebrate my ridiculousness?" I wondered.

"Nowhere!"

"Oh stop it," I said, "you love it. Just let me shower you with attention."

"Oh my god," Ayala buried her face in her hands, "I can't tell if you're for real or not."

"It's happening," I said, "just embrace it."

From that moment on it was like a door opened, no more barrier between us. In that space, something wonderful blossomed. Right away I called it '*love.*' Ayala called it '*infatuation.*' Not only that, I got her to admit, she also called it '*a special connection.*'

An infatuated connection sounded like an admittance of love to me. Even if she complained about me a lot:

"You have to stop giving me gifts."

"Does that mean you don't like it?" I frowned.

"It's—it's beautiful," she took the necklace I bought her out of its box.

"Try it on!"

"Okay, okay," she brought it around her neck and picked up her hair, waiting. It took me a moment to realize what she wanted. I stood behind her and closed the clasp, her hair brushing my fingertips.

"What do you think?" Ayala turned to me, the gold Israel charm resting between her collar bones.

"It's so much better on you."

"You're ridiculous," Ayala grinned. She made me laugh.

"I could be more ridiculous," I warned.

More ridiculous? Over the weeks I dropped notes in her backpack reminding her that I care and prepared us lunch for long school days, I surprised her with tickets to the ballet at the Bima that I knew she wanted to see.

She was ridiculous too. Ridiculously smart and thoughtful and beautiful. She started writing me cards and my heart melted just seeing her curly handwriting.

She wrote that I'm special, that she never met anyone like me, anyone so dedicated and caring and thoughtful. She wrote that she's sorry she's not at my speed, but she's getting there, it takes her time but when she feels it she knows it's a hundred percent real.

She wrote that she's getting there.

"You guys are the cutest couple," Ayala's roommate said one evening. I was over for dinner and brought my notes— finals were coming up. My job was to translate them, she'd prepare us food. Instead of looking them over, I watched Ayala cook.

"We are, aren't we?" Ayala said.

I froze and looked up from the papers. Ayala smiled at me and I knew finally she was a hundred percent there.

We eventually discussed it:

"So this is love?" she said.

"Is it a disappointment?"

She burst out laughing. We were always laughing when we were together. We tread lightly and delicately, even in the heaviest of topics.

"Not at all," she said and repeated, "So this is love."

"I thank Hashem every day that I have you."

"Stop."

"Why? You really are the best thing that ever happened to me. And we get to be with each other every day," I paused, "I don't want to scare you—"

"Hey! I'm not so easily scared."

"Okay then," I shrugged, "when are we getting engaged?"

"What?"

"I mean, when would you want to? If you don't know yet... I'll ask you in a few weeks."

"No! I mean I want to. Of course, I want to," she said and added with a wink, "I just don't know you yet."

I took out my cell phone and found the calendar, showing her with my finger, "this is the first day of school." I moved my finger a week down, "this is our first date." I slid the month by, "over here you told me you like me." I moved down a few days, "here I told you straight up how I feel." I swiped another month over, "remember you met my family here?" and another, "time flies. We've known each other for nearly four months."

Finally, Ayala said, "I don't want any ridiculous rings."

It came up almost at random. We were sitting on campus talking about someone else, other circumstances: a friend of a friend who went through a difficult time during the army. He was hospitalized for a few weeks during his service and immediately demoted.

"The army neglects its soldiers' mental health and then punishes them for it," Ayala shook her head.

"Well, what should they do?" I shrugged, "they can't have a bunch of crazies in those intense units. Besides, if they're too sensitive they won't be helpful and they'll mess themselves up even more."

"Is that what you think?" Ayala jumped up, "someone who has a breakdown is '*crazy*.'"

"They're definitely not... normal."

"I can't tell if you're serious or not."

"What? That guy went to a mental institution. *Mental*," I repeated, "you think that's normal?"

"I guess I'm just a 'crazy' to you," she grabbed her bag and started walking away.

"Ayala!" I called and followed her.

We never fought before. I followed her and asked her to explain. She coldly told me she had a breakdown three years ago when she was under a lot of pressure from a lot of things. She was hospitalized. She's fine now, on medication and she feels great. Normal.

A hundred, million percent normal.

"You never told me."

"I didn't think it was a big deal," she said but the way she said it, folded arms and looking away, I knew that she knew it was a big deal.

Anyways, I lied, "it's not a big deal at all. You're you. The same you. Amazing and awesome and beautiful and wonderful and definitely crazy—" I paused, "in the best of ways."

"Of the two of us, it is very clear who's the crazy one in this relationship."

We laughed because we knew it was me. Our first fight passed smoothly and we didn't talk about it again.

That didn't mean I didn't think about it.

Ayala. My beautiful soon-to-be wife. I hadn't properly proposed yet but I ordered a ring. My family was thrilled. My sister fell in love with her the second they met. Ayala had that effect on people.

Ayala. On pills, for problems no one could see. Secret pills, hidden problems.

We went out and Ayala said, "Why are you so quiet?"

We went out and fought more. Argued about nothing and Ayala said, "What is up with you? You're so tense, everything is setting you off."

And I wondered what set her off. What kind of stress is too much stress? What kind of stress will drive her overboard? Hospitalization, medication, these terms were over my head but my mind wandered. Will it happen after we have one kid? What about after the second? Will she break down on me in ten years? In five?

Ayala turned into a time bomb, ticking, ticking away our normal, good times.

What set her off? Too much stress. Three years ago. Is that why she moved? To get away from 'too much'? Will she leave me if she breaks down again, just to 'get away'?

These questions came from all directions. Bombarded me when I was alone, when I was with her, during lectures, when I texted her goodnight and lay awake in bed.

When I told her that I loved her and when we jotted down plans for the near future: potential wedding dates and where we'd live...

It was too much and eventually, I left the one last note in her notebook:

Ayala,

I am so sorry. It's not you, it's me. I am an idiot and a loser and really ridiculous for giving you up but I don't think this is right for me.

Class became unbearably awkward. I sat in the back, she sat in the front. I watched her play with her long blond hair and hated myself for letting her go and hating her for not being who I thought she was.

How to Ace a Date

I cursed to myself and ran down the block to my car. I should have left a half hour ago, I should have been home right now, showering, putting on a fresh shirt and clean pants. I looked down at my polo shirt. It was fine, a little stained but nothing major. Also, earlier I'd sweat a ton, down in the basement working on wiring.

I'm an electrician, it isn't the easiest job, I thought as I sniffed my armpits—not bad. It's mentally and physically challenging and she'd just have to respect that I'm hardworking. She herself said she wants a working guy.

Once in my car, I took a few deep breaths, turned the radio on and relaxed for a nice couple of minutes. It isn't healthy to jump straight from work to the date, no reason to rush, I had to clear my mind first.

It was my first date with Simmy Weingarten and I arrived at her door twenty minutes late. Not bad, and I was a hundred percent focused.

"Hi," Simmy opened the door and smiled.

Nice teeth, could use a whitening though, long hair—the smooth kind—skinny too. She looked good. I warmly greeted her back.

In the car, I had the courtesy to ask like I always did, "Where do you want to go?"

"Whatever you want," she said. Of course. Girls these days have no opinions, Simmy was no different.

I took her to my favorite pizza shop. It was in the area, cheap, but still had the best food in town.

"This is very local," she said as I chose toppings.

"What do you want?" I said, "One or two?"

I got three for myself.

"Just one," she said and I nodded approvingly. That's how she stays so darn thin.

Once our slices were warm, we sat in a booth. Simmy insisted we sit in the one in the farthest corner.

"So you do know what you want, eh?" I joked.

"What?"

Another problem, girls don't get jokes. I sighed and folded my slice.

"I didn't eat all day," I explained before I took a bite. Saucy cheese dripped on my cheek. It was perfect.

She ate her slice a fork and knife, no joke! She cut tiny squares and chewed each one slowly.

"You always on a diet?" I asked.

"I'm not on a diet."

"Don't be embarrassed," I said, "it's a good thing. I'd rather my wife be on a diet. Y'know? All these dieting couples get married and a year later they both blow up. Now it's fine for a guy, but I hate when women do that."

She stared at me.

"Not that I think you'd do that!" I rushed, "it's just... good you're dieting. Good for you."

After a few nibbles of pizza, I already started my second, she said: "I wouldn't want my husband to get fat either."

I laughed.

"Kay," I started, now that the ice was broken we could really begin to get to know each other, "so this is your first date?"

"Ever?"

"No, with me," I rolled my eyes, "yes, ever."

She shrugged, "well, I've gone out a couple of times before. Nothing serious—"

"How many?"

"What?"

"How many times have you gone out? You have to know. Five, ten?"

"A few... a lot! I don't know."

Definitely over ten. Maybe even over twenty. Damn, this girl's been in the field for a while.

"How long was the longest you went out for?"

She shrugged again, "I don't know, a month, two?"

"You were *shomer negiah* the whole time?"

"What are you asking me?"

I didn't press. That meant she wasn't. I wondered how far she went with that dude. I wondered who ended it and why. We were only on a first date though, so I let the questions slide for now.

"I went out with a few girls. There was one that was really hot, but a complete airhead. You know the type?"

"No."

"Here, let me find her on Facebook to show you." I dug out my phone and tried to remember her last name.

"It's fine. I really don't need to see—"

"Jacobson!" I remembered and typed her name.

"Wow," I looked through her pictures, "you'd never believe it, she's married now."

She looked even better in a wig, "what do you think?" I showed Simmy.

"Very pretty."

She smiled thinly and I could tell she was jealous.

"Don't worry, you're pretty too."

I folded the third slice and bit in.

"This is going well, isn't it?"

Simmy nodded.

"I like that you're easygoing. You're a bit quiet though, aren't you?"

"I don't know what to say."

"Really?" I challenged and finished the slice in four bites.

"Well, maybe we should get going."

The pizza was all sliced up but she barely ate any of it, "You're not finished eating."

"I'm not hungry."

I pulled her plate towards me and popped the little chunks in my mouth.

"You're right," I said, "I am *exhausted.*"

We went out to the car. I drove for a minute and sighed deeply. Of course, gas was low. We went to fill up and I told her all about my job.

"You work too, right?" I said once we were near her house.

"Yes."

"Awesome. So… you're free Tuesday night?" I put the car in park.

"No."

"Wednesday?"

"I'll—I'll check."

"Great, let me know!" I grinned.

The next day the *shadchan* called.

I already told my mother I had a great time.

"We could go out Wednesday," I told her to say.

My mother hung up frowning, "Simmy isn't interested."

"Are you serious?" I was shocked and hurt, "What's her number? I'll call her myself. She told me she was!"

"I'm so sorry," my mother said, "she's really missing out."

166

Bubbeh Maises

It's good to be open-minded. That's what everyone is saying at least; that our grandparents have this limited view on the world, they never change so they're all stuck with their *bubbeh maises*. Our generation knows better. We know not to judge books by their covers, that nothing is really as it seems.

I'm all about keeping up with the times. To prove it, I even went out with a girl like Shirel.

167

Shirel had gone to high school with my sister, they were in different classes but my sister knew her well enough and only had great things to say. Shirel was pretty—if you like dark hair and dark eyes and dark skin which I didn't mind much, she was smart and talkative too, studying in college with a full scholarship.

Also, she was Moroccan.

As I said, I'm open-minded. It was not a big deal at all.

The first date we went out to a decent café. Sitting across from her, I was pleasantly surprised to see no hair on her upper lip. Relieved even. Her coffee colored arms were smooth and hairless as well.

We spoke about our family backgrounds—my grandparents were Hungarian, came to New York during the war. Hers were fully Moroccan, born and raised in Casablanca. I wondered how they managed to get along in this first world country, but I didn't ask. Shirel seemed fully adjusted anyways. We spoke about Pesach too, as it was two weeks away. As usual, my family was going to a hotel because my mother had a hard time cooking Pesach food. Her family was staying at home.

"Oh!" I just remembered, "Well it's not really Pesach for you, is it? You could basically eat whatever you want."

She shrugged, "I mean, I'll definitely miss bread, but I'll be okay."

"Yeah, but rice! Imagine, you could eat regular cookies!" I shook my head, this girl did not know how lucky she was, how other Jews suffered the full week from potato starch overload, "your Pesach is totally fake, I'm telling you."

"You're right. I'll tell my family to call off the cleaning. It's all a scam."

It took me a moment to realize she was joking and I laughed along. Oh, Shirel. Funny girl.

Our date went well, conversation flowed, she had a good sense of humor and good nature, so naturally, we went out again.

Our second date and our conversation deepened surprisingly quickly.

We spoke about culture and language.

"How do you say, 'have a good day,' in Moroccan?" I wondered.

"You mean Arabic?"

"Yeah, exactly," I said, while in my head I was reeling. Her family was Jewish, weren't they? Not Arabic. I couldn't make sense of it so I pushed my thoughts aside and focused on Shirel.

She shrugged, "how would I know how to speak it?"

"You don't speak Moroccan?" I was surprised.

"Do you speak Hungarian?"

"No."

"See?"

"Yeah, but you *are* Moroccan."

She didn't argue back but I could tell she wanted to. I could tell under her thick skin, aggression was pulsing through her veins. It's something I'd have to accept, I realized if I wanted it to work out with her.

"You can be angry, I understand."

"I'm not angry though."

I rolled my eyes. It was the most passive-aggressive sentence she could use and she used it at least once on every date.

Still, hanging out with Shirel was fun. She was so exotic and foreign. She had a surprisingly good family too. On the following date, I asked all the indirect questions I could to find out about her parents. Well, more about her father really. If he hit the mother and all that. I wouldn't want Shirel coming from such an environment of fear. It could, G-d forbid, cause her to expect me to act as horribly to her.

I asked questions like: "Do you like Shabbos meals?"

"Of course. It's really the only time all week that my whole family gets together. It's really fun."

170

And: "Who are you closer to, your mother or father?"

"Wow. It's really hard to say. I guess my father. He's really open and warm—not that my mother isn't," she laughed. I was pleased.

Two nights before Pesach we planned to get together.

"I'm not sure where we can go," I said honestly over the phone the night before, "the restaurants are all crazy."

"We don't have to eat out," she said, "I could prepare something and we can go anywhere."

I was about to agree, thinking about all the potato and egg and nothing else that we had at home and all the grains that *she* must have—but then I remembered, "Nah, it's fine. It's not really my taste, you know."

"What isn't? My cooking?" she sounded offended.

I quickly corrected myself, "No! Don't get me wrong. You must be great—actually, you are *for sure* great. I'm just a bit sensitive to spicy food..."

"And...?"

"You're right. Make whatever. It's fine. I'll bring extra water and—" I was about to say bread and realized, "Actually! You could bring rice... without anything on it, is that fine?"

"I don't cook spicy food."

I laughed. She didn't laugh with me.

"What do you mean?" I said

"I'm not so into spicy food either," she said.

"Oh." I paused and smiled, "great."

We went to the zoo and ate great fake Pesach food.

"This is way better than I expected!" I exclaimed as I ate. And I realized, I love Sephardis and all of their lenient *minhagim.*

It was going so well, on the way back home I mentioned, "I didn't check Dor Yesharim but its fine. You're Sephardic anyways."

"I actually heard it's important to check regardless."

"Nope," I laughed, "it doesn't work like that."

"I'd want to check anyway," she said, "just to make sure."

"Relax Shirel, you don't have to get so riled up," Oy. I never knew what would set this hot-headed girl off. I had to be careful around her.

"I'm not, I'm just telling you what's important to me."

Under her words, I sensed her seething.

I called her up on *Erev Yontif.* It felt wrong to break the news so suddenly, and right before Pesach of all days, but my parents told me it was better. This way I wouldn't keep her wondering the next two days straight. Still... I didn't want her to go into *Yontif* hurt and sad.

I took a deep breath and made the call.

172

"This isn't going to work out," I said, "I feel like we argue too much. You know what I'm talking about, right?"

"I was thinking the same thing," Shirel said and thanked me pleasantly and wished me good luck.

Underneath her leveled tone I felt all that pent up rage and aggression and was relieved I dodged this bullet. No more open-mindedness for me. From now on only Ashkenazi girls.

Mr. Perfect

I knew from the start it was too good to be true. He was twenty-four years old, a law school graduate, interning at a high up firm while waiting to take his bar exam, intelligent and put together. The best part—he was tall! So tall, over six feet. I used to say I didn't care about height, but sometime during the years of dating tiny guys and feeling like a giant in all my five feet eight inches I developed a resentment.

How many years of dating? I did the calculation, from my first date at eighteen, I'm twenty-eight now... a whole lot of years. But in all honesty, I wouldn't call this past year 'dating.' I was only set up with one guy since Rosh Hashana, he was almost forty and had two kids.

"What can I tell you?" The *shadchan* said, unsympathetically, "You're getting older, your options are limited. If I were you I'd take what I can get..."

I hung up, took a breath, and regretted acting angry. One more *shadchan* that wouldn't set me up again.

But now this... this catch—Shimon Gottlieb. We were matched on *SawYouAtSinai*, I double and triple checked to see that he already agreed to go out, it was up to me. Did I have a choice? I almost *challished* just looking at his photo. His broad shoulders and perfect dimples—perfection.

After the first date my parents were already judging my dreamy expression, they sang all the wedding songs they knew until I yelled at them to stop.

"You're making an *ayin hara*!" I said, "I don't even know what he's thinking. What if he doesn't want to go out again?"

Shimon wanted to go out again.

"It would be his pleasure," the *shadchan* said.

The second date went better than the first, we went on a ferry and watched the city and spoke about our goals.

"I see all these people following *halacha* on autopilot..." Shimon said and shook his head, "That's not what I want. I want a strong *frum* home out of love, I want my family to love Torah," he shrugged and smiled, those dimples drilling gorgeous holes in his cheeks.

"That's what I try teaching my students. That it's not about all of this," I gestured grandly at the city, the people—the physical world we get so caught up in, "it's about the connection and love."

He nodded slowly and I sighed in relief from his approval. Everything he said sounded deep and thoughtful. The way he squinted his eyes into the distance and spoke in a low voice. The voice I had to lean in to hear, each word intriguing me more. My voice sounded shallow in comparison.

By the third date my parents' excitement was infectious, I was already making calculations in my own head. Two months till engagement... three months from then. We could be married by Sukkos!

No, no. This wasn't good. I had to calm down. Three dates didn't mean much. When I was twenty I went out with a boy for over a month. He was stylish and charming and I had never felt as comfortable with anyone else—so I told him. I thought I'd marry him. I wasn't the stylish wife he wanted me to be. I would have changed for him, but out of nowhere he broke it off, said it won't work out, sorry for wasting my time.

Since then I tried not to get my hopes up dating. Not that there have been many chances to get my hopes up. I had semi-serious month of dating again at twenty-four, I thought I'd marry him too. And that was it. The waiting game.

Why should a guy like Shimon be into me anyways?

I'm the kind of girl that you meet and forget about. Blond hair, skin so pale you can practically see through it. Went to a decent sem, got a decent degree, volunteered in the same camps as everybody else, teach at a Bais Yaakov, go to Zumba and spinning classes three times a week, even wrote the same dating resume like everyone else: I'm a good girl, I want a decent guy. I'm not asking for much, just someone who loves me who I can build a home with.

Shimon is the kind of guy that could get so much better. He can get funny and cool, rich and stunning. He himself seemed to make nice money, judging by his watch and car and sunglasses.

"I'm happy with my job," he said, "but the hours are long so I can't learn as much as I'd like to."

We spoke over dinner at a steakhouse in Manhattan. Shimon ordered steak and I ordered a salad. His dish looked so appetizing but I pretended to chew my lettuce enthusiastically. My father told me it's not feminine to order steak. Women get salads.

"Oh, stop it. Get what you want," my mother told me, "just don't finish everything on your plate. You'll look like a *chazer*."

I moved the tomatoes around my bowl and Shimon surprised me. He asked, "what's wrong?'

"Why do you think something is wrong?"

"You have no appetite," he said, "are you sure you just want a salad?"

I was about to shake my head and say I was fine but something inside stopped me, "actually is it too late to order a steak too?"

"Eat from my plate and we'll get more," he pushed his plate to the center of the table.

It spread from my head to toes, this tingling relief. I stuck my fork into his meat and he sliced it for me neatly.

He said he wanted to see me during the day, not just evenings, so on Sunday, he picked me up with a surprise plan.

We drove an hour to a state park I'd never been to. He was surprised, "my family used to come here all the time when we were kids."

Of course, the perfect family too. I smiled and cringed at the same time because the more perfect he was, the more inadequate I felt with him. His perfection just drew a bigger gap between us.

He opened the trunk and unpacked a blanket and cooler.

"You didn't tell me to bring anything!" I said as we set up the contents of the cooler on our picnic blanket. A container of salad, one of rice, one of something too complicated to decipher, and one of cookies. Orange juice, lemonade, water, champagne.

"Don't worry, I have everything we need."

Lunch was fantastic. Shimon opened the champagne and I drank and I shouldn't have. It made me giggle, imagining Shimon in a little apron cutting cucumbers into cubes. I grew hot and blushed. The park was too empty for this. We were alone on this blanket in an endless field of grass, an hour from home and I drank the full cup of champagne.

"Did you bake these?" I said after trying a cookie. No way could he bake too. It wouldn't be fair—my cookies burn, come out too sugary sweet or too bland, I can never get them right. These cookies were soft and chewy and perfectly chocolatey.

"It's my aunt's recipe," he shrugged, such a childish gesture for such manly shoulders. He wore a light polo shirt today so I got the full view of his shoulders and arms. They were so defined, I could make out every muscle—

"Do you work out?" I blurted out and blushed again. The sun was really bright, of course, I was feeling hot. We should have chosen a spot in the shade.

"I train at Barry's Bootcamp," he said, "you heard of it?"

I didn't but whatever he did, it worked. At least I didn't tell him that. If I did, I'd blush so deep my blood vessels would burst.

"What about you?"

I told him about boring Zumba and boring spinning but he seemed impressed.

"So you must be a really good dancer."

"Yep..." I said, "I'll show you sometime," I winked and felt risky for doing it, but also confident and frisky.

He laughed uncomfortably and I worried I crossed the line. So many dates over the years, I was forgetting dating etiquette. At what point was flirting allowed? Was it ever allowed? Was what I did even considered flirting?

I stopped with the champagne and chugged water instead.

Our next date was in the evening, at a formal restaurant, he wore a button-down shirt. It was fitted but not like his polo. I dressed in a nice dress and expensive perfume, see Shimon? I could be formal too.

"You think he's going to propose?" My mother asked when I got home. I shrugged nonchalantly when really I had already imagined twenty scenarios of Shimon popping the question.

Still no proposal, but we went out a whole lot. We went to quirky restaurants, museums, movies, and shows. Nothing too private again, he knew it was dangerous. I made sure not to order wine, even though I'd order steak and finish the whole thing.

One night, strolling in Central Park, he told me—and my heart fluttered—"you're so distracting, did you know?"

And I was so distracted by his eyes, boring down into mine. For a second I thought he'd kiss me. What should I do? My thoughts raced, should I stop him, the good *shomer* girl that I was? Should I let him? What would my students say? I really wanted to let him.

But the moment passed and nothing happened. He cleared his throat and asked if I was okay.

Weeks passed. We continued dating. I continued doubting my luck while falling deeper for him. He seemed to really like me, he told me nice things—that he liked how I matched my shoes to my purse, how I'm a perfect listener and I make him think. That he feels like we're open with each other and that's a really good basis for a relationship.

I wasn't open to him about my dreams. He showed up in them, more than once. It was even starting to become a problem, waking up in the morning and keeping my eyes shut in hopes that bits of the dream will come back. I held onto what I could. I came late to class so much, the principal noticed.

And then came the day. My heart swelled, he brought it up—engagement.

We'd spoken about it before of course, but more theoretically. Now we spoke *tachlis*: when, where, what.

That night, at home my parents sang wedding songs at the top of their lungs...and I sang along with them.

He told me on the phone, it's easier this way, he said, and, I don't think I could tell you in person. My heart cracked. It all happened in the course of a phone call:

"I haven't been completely honest with you."

I waited.

"I really love you, I'll always love you. That won't change."

"Are you breaking up with me?"

"I'm giving you a choice," he took a shuddering breath, and the line got static-y. It took me a moment to realize he was crying.

"Shimon, what happened? You can tell me." It was another woman. I already knew. Someone rich and sexy enough (I realized slowly and then shockingly clear that I'd never been sexy enough for him), he found someone smart and philosophically deep just as he liked. I'm just a simple girl, what do I know? I felt my cheeks wet too. It was stupid. I was almost happy he admitted it, I shouldn't be crying. Happy because I expected this all along, was just waiting for him to outright say it—I am not good enough for him.

"Please don't hate me," he whispered, "please don't." If this was in person and not over the phone, I'd have to lean in to hear, lean in and catch a hint of his cologne. It was Ralph Lauren and he wore it so well. How many times did I dream of him holding me? My head in his chest inhaling the scent of Shimon and Ralph Lauren, the perfect combo.

"I could never hate you," I said and it was true. If I were hotter and smarter this wouldn't happen, I'd be able to keep him. He'd be mine.

"I'm not sexually attracted to you," he said, his voice turned distant, "I'm so sorry, I'm so sorry." He kept repeating.

Suddenly I was angry. The tears turned hot and fast, "Who is it then? Who's sexy enough for you? Is it a secretary from work? Some shiksa from the gym? Are you already with her?

Do you kiss her?" I took a deep breath, shocked at myself. Too riled up to feel regretful and embarrassed yet.

He said my name, said it again, "it's not that. Oh God, it's not that at all." He paused and the weight of the universe passed in that pause, "I'm gay. I'm sorry. I am so sorry. I am horrible, but everything I ever said to you was true. I love you, you're captivating. You intrigue me. You make me think and you make me happy."

My heart didn't just crack. It splintered and now he rubbed the dust of it into the ground with the sole of his shoe.

"I love you so much, I'm telling you to leave me. But I also love you and I still want to marry you. I want to live a religious life, I believe in God, that he gives everyone their challenges. I want a family, I want to be normal. I want to go to therapy, I want to get through this." He didn't give me a chance to speak, not that I was capable of speaking, "I understand you, whatever you do. You don't know how sorry I am. Yell at me, leave me, cut me off... marry me. Whatever you want. I really do love you..."

I hung up and cried. I cried until my eyes puffed red and my head pounded. Then I went downstairs, had a bowl of cereal, called in sick for the rest of the week and watched a lot of TV. I watched a reality show about brides picking out wedding gowns. I thought of husbands who bake and husbands in little aprons. I thought of broad shoulders, toned arms and lips that never wanted to kiss me. That would never want to kiss me. Maybe just a courtesy kiss, maybe if I wore his cologne and dressed like a dude. Maybe if we went to therapy and worked and worked and worked through it and never gave up.

Two days later I called Shimon back.

A week later he proposed with a two-carat diamond ring.

Two weeks later, we had the engagement party, a rooftop venue, family, and friends. All of mine showed up with their hubbies and a kid or two or three. They told me they were happy for me, so happy for me. I smiled and looked at their babies and said thank you so much.

We were married before Sukkos. In the pictures, I looked beautiful and petite next to my over six-foot tall man, nice stubble and strong arms. He smiled with his dimples and charm and wrapped those arms around me for the photographer.

He wraps those arms around me at night, for me.

Ready or Not

I want to get married. I really really want it bad. Single life is nice at twenty-one when chilling with the guys in Yeshiva seems more appealing than pleasing a needy wife. Single is also nice at twenty-four when all your friends have to work endless shifts to make enough for diapers and rent. Instead, I'd spend my money on nice cars and nights in Atlantic City.

Single isn't nice at thirty when you're too tired to go out, don't have anyone to go out with, don't even see the appeal in going out anymore. And you're also too tired to go home:

an empty apartment, nothing good on TV and takeout containers. It isn't nice when you go for a Shabbos meal at a friend's house and see a combination of the same single faces that pretend to be whole and independent as if submitting to their lifelong sentence of singlehood, as if thirty is the endgame, the marriage boat has sailed and you're left with friends and a career.

I met Tamara on *JSwipe*. She made it clear on her profile that she was interested in a serious connection that would hopefully blossom into a lifelong partnership. That's fancy words for marriage. I wanted it too.

We met for coffee near Central Park and had nice conversations.

"There's this certain urgency to the city," I told her, "it's inspiring... but also tiring."

"I like it," she said, "It really pushes me to work as hard as I can. I don't think I'd make it this far as an engineer if I'd have lived anywhere else."

"The engineering field is harder on women, right?"

"Nothing is as easy for women, but I don't let that stop me," she shrugged, "even dating. The system makes it so easy for guys. All they need to do is tuck in their shirts and act like a mensch."

I looked at my shirt tucked neatly into my pants and didn't say anything about the years I spent searching.

I liked her, I decided after we parted ways. She was intelligent and determined and looked just like the pictures she put up, (you can never trust those flattering selfies).

We met up again a few days later in a restaurant. I'd have met up with her sooner but she worked late nights in the office:

"I'm a woman," she explained, "If I don't work hard, no one will take me seriously."

She came to the date straight from work, her hair frazzled from the day's stresses, bags forming under her eyes. She assured me she was fine, not tired at all, really happy to meet with me again.

We ordered a few appetizers. And a bottle of wine, Tamara made sure to add.

Conversation with her was like pulling on a loose thread, hard to find but once discovered, endless in depth. We spoke about vacations, we both liked those.

"I like to travel somewhere new every year," she said, using her twelve vacation days on the trip. She'd been to Thailand and China and England and France and Brazil. She used to be afraid to travel alone but got used to it. Now she can't imagine traveling any other way.

I was different, I liked to use my vacation in little bursts when I felt like I really needed them, extended weekends away with friends, not usually farther than upstate in the summer and Miami in the winter. The farthest I'd traveled was to Israel on Birthright nearly a decade ago.

"Typical," she smiled.

"What's wrong with typical?"

She shrugged, "if you always do the same thing, how could you ever change?"

We ordered main dishes and I told her to choose for me. Tonight was a night of changes, I announced. It would be interesting to travel to a foreign country, something I'd like to do with my wife.

We were testing the food, sipping wine, commenting to each other and enjoying that there was someone else to comment to, when Tamara said, "So, what's your story?"

It felt like a trick question, so I trod carefully, "in regards to..?"

"You seem like a nice guy," She looked me up and down, "why aren't you married yet?"

I paused. It was the kind of question I'd ask myself countlessly, I'd ask God countlessly, but no one would ask me. Because the answer to it is glaringly obvious and the lack of an answer is sad.

"I just haven't found a girl for me—"

"—*woman*. You mean woman."

"Yes, of course. I haven't found the woman for me."

"You've been looking?"

"More seriously as I got older," I said honestly, "but it's not always easy finding someone who really gets you and shares your values... as you must know." If you're twenty and married you think it's easy. When you're thirty and unmarried, you know it's hard.

She shook her head, "it still doesn't add up. You're a guy. You have all the options, all you have to do is choose."

All the options? I added up all the girls—no, *women* that I really connected with in my entire dating life. There was Kayla, but she said I'm not religious enough and I said she was too closed-minded. There was Adina, who always had what to say but I felt didn't like much what I had to say. There was Esther, who was perfect and beautiful and kind but she said she can't continue because she was in love with somebody else, her ex-boyfriend that she couldn't get over no matter how hard she tried. They got married less than a year later. What was the choice here?

"Well, I haven't chosen yet," I said finally. I didn't want to talk about this anymore. I didn't want to ask her why she didn't find anyone, the nice girl that she is. I was scared she'd have all the answers even though there was no answer to questions like this and I wasn't in the mood of being blamed, the entitled man that I must be.

I didn't like the Coq Au Vin she ordered for me. I pushed my plate to the center of the table and picked at the appetizers.

Half an hour later she finished too. I gave my card to the waiter and she gave hers.

"Put half on this," she said.

I smiled, "that's how it goes nowadays, eh?"

She nodded, "besides, I don't want to feel like I owe you anything."

It wasn't too late yet but Tamara had to go. She was exhausted from her long day and had to rest up before her long day tomorrow. She had a nice time though. I told her I was happy she feels I'm worth squeezing into her schedule.

We each drove ourselves to our empty homes in our nice cars.

"Are you busy *motzei Shabbos*?" I asked her over the phone later in the week.

"Actually yeah," she said apologetically, "I bought a ticket to *Hamilton* on Broadway. I've been meaning to go for a while..."

"Oh," I frowned and thought, "Maybe I'll meet you after? No, no. You'll be with your friends..."

She laughed, "Actually, I'm going alone. I didn't think I'd have anyone to go with so I just booked myself. I can't spend my whole life waiting for someone."

I agreed, hung up and didn't know how to feel. Tamara was smart and thoughtful and hardworking and... I could've continued all day with great traits I saw in her, but I didn't understand how her great traits fit with me if she was able to fit me into the closed circuit life she created for herself.

Maybe if she understood that I believed in women's rights she'd open up to me. Maybe if she knew I attended an egalitarian *minyan* on Shabbat and asked my female friends if they wanted to make *Kiddush* at our meals she'd like me better.

We were supposed to meet on Sunday but she canceled, we were supposed to meet on Monday but she was too busy. On Tuesday I insisted we go out for lunch. I'll drive to her work.

"It'll only be for an hour," she warned.

A very limited time slot. I prepared the topics of conversation beforehand.

"What are you looking for in a relationship?"

She, of course, had an answer ready, "I want to be in a relationship that only pushed me forward, where we accept each other as individuals and help each other grow."

"I think in every relationship you have to make some compromises," I said. It wasn't always about growing, I knew. Sometimes a relationship could be waiting for someone to catch up, or holding their hand and pulling them up, falling behind as you do. Only because when you need, they'll do the same for you.

"Of course. Think of what I'd have to give up having kids."

"You do want kids, don't you?"

"Yes," she laughed but it sounded scolding, "I don't even have to ask you if you do. It's not your body that will change and swells and sags and go through horrific pain. Nope. You just wait on the side and enjoy the prize."

For some reason, I wanted to apologize, but I held myself back. Apologize for what? For being born male? For biology and the way God created the world?

I gave it one more shot, meeting up for another three-hour dinner date. It was nice and fun and interesting and the day after over the phone I told her, "I don't think this is going to work out."

She didn't say anything and for a second I thought she hung up, but then she said coldly, "I'd expect you to at least have some decency to tell me to my face, we've been going out for a few weeks already."

I didn't mention that over those few weeks we've seen each other a grand total of four times and that if I wanted to break up with her in person I'd have to wait another week to do so.

All I said was, "I'm sorry," and, "do you want to talk about this in person?"

"Don't worry about it, I'm a big girl—" *Woman*, I wanted to correct her but didn't, "—I can take care of myself."

She didn't need to tell me twice.

Best Day Ever

The second saddest day of my life was my best friend's wedding. I'm a good friend though, I sat with Tziporah through it all. As she got a crown put into her elaborate curls, as she got eyelash extensions and blush to perfectly contour her cheekbones. She looked more beautiful than I'd ever seen her and inside I seethed with jealousy. I got my makeup done too but no one really paid attention to me.

She *davened* Mincha with so much *kavanah*, but I knew it was fake. She didn't *daven* Mincha any other day of her life.

On my wedding day, I knew, I'd *daven* with real *kavanah*. At her chuppah, I cried but it was fine because everyone cries. The rest of the time I had to smile and dance. Only afterward, in bed with my face blotched with stubborn makeup and the band music ringing in my ears was I able to properly break down. This wasn't just my best friend. This was my *last* friend, we relied on each other for evening plans and Shabbos hangouts. My *last* single friend.

Now I was truly and fully alone on this horrid island of singleness.

The first saddest day of my life was my little sister's wedding. She was eighteen and innocent and had no *hakaras hatov* for how lucky she was. Yitzy was the first boy she ever went out with and of course, things worked out perfectly. They got engaged a month after, organized the wedding within the next two. She glowed with happiness the whole time. As if *that* wasn't enough, she scolded *me* about it:

"Why can't you just be happy for me?"

Excuse me?!

The worst part—no one even asked me if I cared that my baby sister was getting married before me. What happened to good old fashioned sensitivity? I didn't have to pretend to smile and jump with excitement this time. She's the one that had to be sensitive to me. I'm twenty-one years old and she knew I have been searching for years.

So here I am, months later, still single, waiting in my childhood bedroom and wishing I could have my own home instead. I really have a knack for decoration and I've been wanting to redo my room but logic always told me to wait. No point in putting in the effort if anyways I'm moving out soon.

... Except what happens when 'soon' turns from months to years? When the baby pink paint on the wall fades and peels with time?

What happens when you don't get married when you expect to?

I've read about *it* in magazines. Hard not to when fear is sweeping the community, when every girl you know bites their fingers in their homes waiting for *shadchanim* to call. I've heard all too much about the horrid *shidduch crisis.* And slowly, I realized, I was becoming that dreaded statistic.

When Pinchas Bernstein was *redt* to me he sounded okay, not really my type. His family didn't have money and Pinchas didn't have a degree. But his friends said he had good *middos* and his rabbi said he was a gem of a boy.

"Okay," I told my mother, "he sounds great! I'll go out with him."

Our first date was a pleasant sort. He spoke a little about his family. I told him about mine, sounding genuinely happy for my married little sister just like I practiced. He was a good listener.

We went out again. I told him about the kind of living room I'd like to have. A cross between old-fashioned and modern. Perhaps with a touch of nature. He said he thought it was a nice idea.

Our next date he told me about yeshivas he thought would be good for kids. That's the husband's area to choose, I nodded to whatever he said.

The wife gets to choose the tablecloth for the Shabbos table and the candlesticks from the catalog. The wife also chooses the bedding for the master bedroom and what kind of wardrobe the babies should have.

He liked simple foods like schnitzel and baked potato. That was fine, as long as I got to cook fancy recipes too.

It was almost too easy. *And* too fast. A week and a half later we were sitting with our parents clinging glasses. His family couldn't afford a ring.

"That's okay, right?"

I nodded somberly, unable to look him in the eye.

He quickly added, "Maybe in a few years we'll get one."

198

"It's fine," I assured him, as long as we were officially engaged.

The most surreal moment was seeing our picture on *OnlySimcha's.* Me and the stranger of a boy at my side. Under two weeks ago we met and now we were destined to each other for life.

"OMG!" Tziporah gushed over the phone, "Tell me all about him!"

I laughed, "I don't know what to say."

"I don't know... what about his family, how many siblings does he have?"

"Um..." I wracked my brain, "Definitely a lot. I haven't met them all yet so it's hard to remember."

"What does he do?"

"He works in... financing," I made up. It sounded good. I'd have to ask him all of this when I saw him. I switched the topic, "the wedding is in March."

"So soon!"

"I know!" Just a month away and right before Pesach. If we would have pushed it off any longer, we'd have had to wait until after *sfira* and that was just too long. "I got the same makeup artist you had. She did such a good job, didn't she? We're deciding what kind of flowers we want. He's very easygoing so it's more up to me."

We spoke for hours about wedding plans. Tziporah was such an amazing friend, I realized, and she had great planning advice. It was really *min hashamayim* she had to go through it all first. She left me with a list of the top videographers.

Our engagement party was in a hall. It was so grand compared to my little sister's party. Hers had been in our living room. I wondered if she was jealous of the grand centerpieces on the tables and the catered dinner. It made me angry. Didn't she get that I deserved this party? I waited longer than she would ever know.

Pinchas and I posed for pictures together and then I spoke to all our guests. His parents, his sister and brother, (he only had two siblings!) his aunts and cousins. There were so many people to meet. It was quite overwhelming.

"I am so happy for Pinny," his bubby said.

"Who's Pinny?" I wondered.

She gave me a look and said again, "Pinny, our Pinny!"

"Oh," I realized and laughed, "Pinchas."

"Yes, we all call him Pinny."

I shrugged and moved on to speak to other people.

The following weeks were so hectic. I had so much to do: pick out a sheitel, a fall, last minute a *WunderWig* too, find an apartment, choose furniture, and attend *kallah* classes.

I barely even had time to spend with my *chosson*, we were both so busy. There was so much to do!

The best day of my life: my wedding day of course. It arrived faster than I expected. The whole day passed in a dreamlike frenzy. The hair, the makeup. I had a tiara in my beautiful hair.

"You look amazing!" my little sister told me and I gave her a hug. Sometime during the past two months my anger towards her disintegrated and now I just felt love towards her.

I *davened* the best Mincha of my life, whispering the names of all the unfortunate singles that I knew. I, of all people, knew just how hard it was. I really thought I'd stay in that ugly pink bedroom until forty but look who's wearing the wedding dress now! I thanked Hashem a thousand times.

Next came pictures. I knew the exact poses I wanted, no wonder the photographer was so impressed.

And then came the best part, I was sitting in the *kallah*'s chair—*me!*— and my *chosson* puts my veil on. My parents lead me to the chuppah after him.

I stood under the canopy under the stars and blinked back tears so my makeup wouldn't smudge. It was *me* under the chuppah. Not Tziporah nor Gitty nor Chana nor Eliana.

Me, myself and I. *My* turn to get married. My turn to start my life as a married woman.

Best day ever.

Anonymous Post

I don't know who to go to for advice. I'm getting married I"H next month and I don't know if I want to. I mean, of course, I do want to… I just don't know if I should. I really don't know what to do.

I'll start from the beginning: I'm in my thirties, I've been in the shidduch scene for years, so many years I've nearly given up. It's disheartening, the advice I get from friends and family. They tell me to go out more and dress up, to stop studying all the time. I'm a doctor and I'm proud of myself.

My father would always say it's not a job for a woman. I ignored his sexist views and persisted. My three sisters are housewives, they shop for groceries and clean the house, spend periods of bed rest through hard pregnancies bombarding our WhatsApp group with complaints about backaches and false alarm trips to the hospital.

At work my co-workers admire me. My face is on the chart for employee of the month, my patients smile when they see me and I really make a difference. They all know I work my hardest. With my family, I feel like a failure. Yomim tovim at home are the hardest, sitting at the extended table with my parents, sisters, their husbands, and children. They all compare their kids' school reports and mysterious viruses and earaches that had them worrying. The only thing worse is when they are away with their in-laws or on vacation and I don't have time to make plans with friends. I sit at the table with just my parents and they try to ask about my work but they are too far removed.

I've always wanted children, husband or not, I wanted nothing more. But I was scared to do it myself, scared of what the community would say—scared that my child would blame me for not having a father. And scared for myself, that I would lose any chance of ever finding a husband. I was still romantic. I still hoped for love.

So I waited.

I waited and hated Hashem and hated myself for hating Hashem. But I did. I hated Him for the challenges he put me through. I didn't deserve it. Why did my friends and sisters deserve marriage any more than me? Were they prettier? Better? Did more mitzvos? I knew it was a toxic way to think but I couldn't stop myself from comparing.

A few months ago, a friend set me up with a guy she knows. He is frum, in his thirties, never married, great job. I was thrilled. We went out and I was even more thrilled. He really understands me and appreciates me exactly as I am. He's intelligent and deep and has really good middos. He's quiet, more of a speculator but I liked that about him. When he proposed I felt a physical weight lift off my heart. Like this was the conclusion to my challenge. The reason I waited so long—to marry THIS man, build a home with HIM and have children with HIM.

A week ago a good friend called me and told me things about this man I'm engaged to marry. Things I didn't know and things I wish I'd never known. I knew he had some sort of past but I didn't imagine this. I didn't know what to imagine so I never asked.

My future husband forced sex upon a woman.

I am engaged to a rapist.

It happened a long time ago. Perhaps he did teshuva since. Is it possible to do teshuva for something like this? Should I break it off and cut off all chances of marriage, family, and children? Should I pretend not to know? Can I pretend not to know?

Old News

All throughout high school my teachers would write on my report cards: "Wise beyond her years." It started before high school though. Even as a kid I'd ask questions I shouldn't have been thinking about. Questions about life, about death, questions like, "what happens to us after we die?" and "if Hashem loves us why does he make us get sad sometimes?" Questions my parents couldn't answer so I had to stop asking.

I was the youngest of eight, six years younger than the sibling above me.

"That's where it's from, we all treat her like she's an adult," my parents explained, because depth was a condition that needed explaining. No one treated me like anything, I wanted to say. My childhood was like growing up as an only child in my empty home except instead of overbearing, overprotective parents, mine were laid back and barely cared.

In school I was too quiet, at home I was too loud. My ideas were too wild and my actions were too tamed. I felt nothing I did was ever right. They'd rather a daughter that went shopping for fun and gossiped over the phone until late. They'd rather a normal daughter.

There was one person who understood me. His name was Hillel and he was a family friend. He started out as my father's business partner, but some time along the years those lines blurred. Hillel's family lived in LA, he had no wife nor kids so he'd eat over by us a lot on Shabbos.

It was like he injected energy into our home every time he came. He made it glow, he made it breathe, turned everything animated and alive: the articles he found interesting in *The New York Times*, a point the Gemara made that he felt is very relevant, and the sources he thought are no longer relevant, recommendations on literature and film. I had long lists to catch up on... and when he left the conversations around the table died and we'd go to sleep. It was just my parents and me after all.

I was fourteen when he started working with my father. Fifteen when he started coming over. I'd steal mascara from my mother's makeup bag and apply it in the bathroom before Shabbos. It's not that I wanted to look prettier, just older. Old enough that he'd see me as a person and realize I have what to say too.

At sixteen he noticed me. I kind of forced him too. It was a Tuesday and he was over. An anomaly. Hillel over on a weekday? Unheard of. I came out to the living room to see what the fuss was about.

They almost closed a business deal, Hillel and my father. They were in the final stages but it looked good. Hillel was over to celebrate, nothing major, not yet, but dinner with champagne. My mother roasted turkey for the occasion.

What occasion? My father always used general keywords when speaking about his work, as if I wouldn't understand specifics. I hated it.

Hillel explained the situation: something about waiting for a stakeholder to negotiate a plan of action. Said stakeholder managed to find a buy-in. Now they were only waiting for it to play out.

I didn't understand completely but I nodded as though I did and the comment Hillel awarded me with was worth it: "Dave," he said to my father, "your daughter is really bright."

If there were any doubts before, now I was sure: Shabbos with Hillel became my favorite time of the week. I'd bask in his attention, the way he'd turn his head, look into my eyes and really listen to what I had to say.

A different night he came over and I was struggling with a book report. It was on *To Kill a Mockingbird* and Hillel had a lot to say. I spend an hour typing *his* words and Mrs. Lieberman wouldn't stop praising me the rest of the semester for my insights.

At nineteen I started dating. I had time between my sparse college schedule. I met with *shadchanim* and wrote a resume that described the type of guy I was looking for. I knew exactly what I wanted: someone like Hillel but twenty years younger. Someone handsome, educated, thoughtful and deep.

So I sat through dates with boys and tried to look them in the eyes and take them seriously.

"Do you like films?" I'd ask.

They'd speak about *Family Guy*.

"Do you read the paper?"

They'd tell me about articles from *The Onion* and 'spot-on' memes.

"You'll find someone," Hillel said so certainly at the Shabbos table when I'd complained about a boy's closed-mindedness, "you'll find someone who really gets you."

How could he be so certain? I wondered. He had never found someone himself. In his thirties? Forties? Never married.

It was actually surprising that Hillel showed up that particular week. More recently his Shabbos visits lessened, dwindled down to once a month, even once every two months. In the beginning, it bothered me. I'd get offended and give him the silent treatment for as long as I could— generally no longer than five minutes.

Now I didn't care. I'd sometimes have plans to go over to friends for the meal, even if I knew he was coming over, not intentionally, but I'd never cancel plans for him. Obviously, I was a little upset; this meant he found better entertainment elsewhere. But mostly, I was happy for him.

I was happy because I had an inkling of suspicion of who this 'better entertainment' was. A girlfriend. What else could it be? I hoped to G-d she was beautiful and caring and retrospective and thoughtful. Someone who'd appreciate

Hillel on every level, not just his handsome face. Hillel deserved the best.

I also deserved the best. So I put myself out there, spoke to my neighbors, friends, aunts, and uncles and told them I was looking. It was awkward but I didn't know what else to do.

"You want someone modern," a *shadchan* told me, "You won't find that kind of boy through me."

I still tried. No harm is done in sitting through sixty minutes with a guy, even when you're sure after the first five minutes that it wouldn't work out. That was my mindset in the beginning. Twenty dates later, twenty-five, the small talk started to wear me thin until it was unbearable.

"They are complaining that you're rude!" my mother said.

"Then they are not for me."

I was twenty already. And then twenty one. And still single and Hillel started coming over more again. The four of us by the Shabbos table, I felt fifteen again and wanted to cry.

My own little rebellion—against who? Myself?—I moved out, across town and with two girls I knew from summer camp. They moved to Brooklyn for the boys. I smirked and didn't break the news to them: they came to the wrong place.

It was empowering and liberating. Waking up early for my morning job. I helped a mom get her two kids ready in

212

the morning and drove them to school. Then I got myself ready, spent the day in classes and stayed up late working on assignments. There were dates in between, I went out for a month with a guy I met in the Hillel House. He was cute and studied literature, but he was also goofy with his big curly hair. Too goofy and I had no patience.

The apartment lasted for four months. Then the bills caught up, I needed sleep, I needed savings and I visited home exactly when my mother made chicken soup. Also, one roommate got engaged and it looked like the second one was close.

I moved back home.

"How are your classes going?" Hillel asked and I felt most at home, his eyes on mine as I explained the classes I liked—the ones about Heidegger and Foucault—and the classes I didn't like—astrophysics was a bore.

"Humanities is much more your thing," Hillel agreed. He studied Liberal Arts in his days, "text me if you need any help in the classes."

"That's cheating," I said, "You'll get me hundreds easily."

"So what? You're allowed to do well."

True to his word, Hillel helped, he came over one evening and sat with me in the living room. My mother made meatloaf and hung around. But then she got bored and left us alone to discuss the essence of the truth and the possibility of many truths.

And true to my word we got a hundred—

"*You* got a hundred," Hillel corrected.

He took me out to celebrate. We went to a restaurant and Hillel looked at the menu, "shall we just have wine or a whole feast?"

"Well," I shrugged, smiling, "this *is* my first hundred of the semester."

"Of course," Hillel said and passed me a menu.

We drank and ate and laughed and I wondered what we looked like to others. Father and daughter or couple?

"How did you end up in business?" I asked.

"As opposed to?" he replied, amused.

"Something more creative. You have such a unique thought process."

"Don't worry, I still think too much," he laughed and continued seriously, "you'd be surprised by how creative I have to be sometimes. Business is really all about creativity. Thinking outside the box."

He drove me home.

"Whoever you end up with is a lucky man." He said with a smile that crinkled his eyes.

I wanted to stay in his car forever but I forced myself out, to the door, up the steps, to my room, shut the door and cried.

I didn't want to think of Hillel, of his wavy hair that turned white at the sides, of the fine lines that formed between his eyes when he thought real hard. Of the things he said that made me think and mostly the way he made me feel.

I didn't want to think of him but he thought of me. Invited me out the following week, and even said, "This is fun. We should make a habit of it." after a silent pause he added, "only if you want."

Our order arrived and I looked at his plate. He ordered a chicken salad, no sides, just water.

"You're just getting that?"

He smiled regretfully, "I can't eat those things anymore."

I looked down at my burger and fries and wondered how it felt to be limited in your own body.

Something was happening between us. Something tangibly right and perfect and wrong and messed up.

I asked him the following week on our 'catch-ups' as he put it. As if we didn't catch up on Shabbos. This was a special sort of catching up though, where we could share how we really feel and talk about things that don't interest my parents.

"How old are you, Hillel?"

"Forty-one."

My father was fifty-seven, he used a cane sometimes and complained about his back. My mother was fifty-five. She grew wide around the middle and never understood pop culture references.

Hillel wasn't at all like that. He was fit, went jogging in the mornings, he was on Facebook, had a tablet and knew how to use a smartphone better than me.

So why did it feel wrong when he texted me throughout the day? When he told me it feels like this is something more than just friendship? That he could stop if I want but he doesn't want to stop. He wants to get to know me, deeper and deeper and truly and fully.

I wanted it, too.

I was scared. Oh, so scared because I knew where this would lead—exactly where I wanted this to lead.

We went out on Monday and I enjoyed. He picked me up from school on Tuesday and I could barely wait for my class to end. Wednesday we met up again. By Thursday it was official. I told my parents to wait in the living room. I had something to tell them.

We came home together and took seats. My parents eyed us, side by side on the couch and talked a little. It felt like foreign ground, like the four of us never sat together before.

"We're going out," Hillel announced.

"Congratulations," my father said to me. He wouldn't look at Hillel.

After pleasantries that seemed light but felt strained, Hillel excused himself, it was getting late, he should go, and left us alone.

My father started, "Don't do this to yourself. Please don't."

"What do you mean?" I played dumb for the first time in my life.

"I know you think you like Hillel a lot, but this is inappropriate. And you're both on completely different paths, different mindsets. I'm telling you."

"We like each other a lot."

He looked at my mother for help but she didn't know what to say, "you don't want a boy more your age?"

"What's the big deal?!" I burst.

"You're twenty-one years old!" my father said, trying to keep his calm, "you are young. You have your whole life ahead of you. I'm telling you, don't do this to yourself."

"I like him," I said in a tiny voice.

"And you'll find someone else and you'll like him too," my father said and corrected himself, "You will *love* him, he will love you."

I nodded, went to my room, messaged Hillel and imagined he was twenty years younger in a way you only can while texting.

We went out. We didn't tell my parents.

A month later, back in my living room, he asked my father for my hand.

"Did he let?" I asked Hillel, scared to hear the answer. Scared that he didn't and I would die of heartbreak, scared that my father let and I'd have no chance of ever finding the young love my father depicted for me.

My father let.

It didn't matter anyway.

I loved Hillel. Hillel loved me.

Silent Agreement

Fifteen is a big number. That's how many girls I've gone out with. *Fifteen!* Craziest part? All have said 'yes' to me.

Definitely an ego boost... but what does it say about *me* that I've rejected all of them? Did it mean I was too picky? I explained each situation to my dating counselor and she said I'm dating well. I'm just a guy who knows what I want—mostly I wanted to get married.

Maybe that's why I was so determined to make things work with Chaya.

Her profile sounded good, her photo looked great. She was skinny and rich and was valedictorian in high school.

She was also painfully shy. This, she hadn't mentioned in her profile but it became apparent within the first five minutes.

"So," I said as we got into the car—well, my *father's* car,—"Are you hungry, or do you just want to get a drink?"

Chaya looked at her hands and shrugged.

"A restaurant then?" it was also my father's credit card and he says I should be generous with girls.

She mumbled something to her hands.

"Huh?"

She repeated more clearly, "A drink is good."

Okay then... I drove to a nice smoothie place that my friend once suggested for dates.

We sat down in a booth with our smoothies and I used my natural charm to break the ice:

"So... come here often?" I sure have. I've been there with at least ten girls so far.

Chaya shook her head and sipped her smoothie through the straw.

I looked around. It was Tuesday and not so busy, that was good. I didn't like when places were too packed. I brought it up with Chaya and asked what she thought.

"Mhmm," she nodded. It's good to agree on things.

It seemed like I'd have to revert to my basic questions. I had a list ready in my head so the conversation would never grow sour. I'm a guy, it's my job to lead the conversation after all.

"How many siblings do you have?"

"Six."

"Me too!" I exclaimed. Chaya didn't react, so I continued, "I'm the oldest. Four brothers and two sisters. The baby is seven. She's so cute. What about you?"

"Middle."

"Oh, nice. My brother and I chill a lot. You know, we're almost the same age. Are you close with any of them?"

Chaya nodded.

"Cool, which one?"

"Libby."

I nodded. I didn't want to seem pressing. Maybe the family was a sensitive topic, still, we had to get through the basics.

"What's your Shabbos table like?"

"It's good."

The answer couldn't have been different if I'd have asked any other question in the world.

"By us, we always share *dvar Torahs* and I think that's very important, even if I was never interested when I was a kid." I continued to explain the foods we have, home cooked chicken and store bought potato kugel, "I like it, but there's nothing like homemade. What about you?"

No answer.

"Would you like another?" I asked when I noticed she finished her drink. Chaya shook her head. I barely started on mine.

"Anyways," I continued after a gulp, "it's nice because it's the time of the week everyone can get together. We used to have supper together every day after school but now we're older. You know? I think it's important to have organized family time."

I paused again to drink and waited for her to speak. She didn't. I put my drink down and continued on about family trips, the importance of husband and wife time too. About favorite vacations I've had and the time I stopped over for a day in Russia.

"All in all, I'm happy I left the airport just for the picture of me with the Kremlin."

Chaya nodded sometimes. She was very agreeable, wasn't she?

I took a deep breath and excused myself to the bathroom. Once, safely in a stall, I pulled out my cell phone and Googled date conversation topics:

> —*What's something I wouldn't guess about you?*
>
> —*What are you most passionate about?*
>
> —*What's your dream job?*
>
> —*What sort of things make you laugh out loud?*
>
> —*If work was no longer an option and you had plenty of money, what would you do all day?*

Perfect. I strutted out of the bathroom confidently.

"Kay, I was thinking," I started as I took my seat again, "what's your dream job?"

"I'm in school for social work."

"Yes... but are you passionate about it?"

Chaya nodded.

"That's good. It's good to like your job... but what if you couldn't work and you had lots of money. What would you do all day?"

"Social work."

"If you *can't* work. It's a hypothetical situation."

She shrugged.

"Fine. Let's talk about things we wouldn't guess about each other. I'll start—I was a vegetarian in high school. All four years! We learned about *shechita* and it really turned me off from meat. Now you go."

"It's personal." Chaya said, and then, "it's getting late…"

"Of course. I'm sorry." She's been sitting a half hour without a drink, fidgeting in her seat. Of course, she wants to go. I felt bad for not picking up the signs earlier. I'm usually good with cues, then again girls usually like me.

I drove her home, making no effort for conversation in the car. It was painfully silent and she stared out her window the whole way. I felt stupid and guilty and awkward.

I dropped her off and said the courteous, "I had a really nice time."

"Bye." She didn't look back.

The second I stepped inside my mother bombarded me with questions, "how did it go? Is she sweet? Do you like her?"

I shrugged, thought of Chaya shrugging and nodding and shaking her head with one-word answers for over an hour so I used my words instead, "She doesn't like me."

"What! I'm sure she does."

"Nope, it's fine. She's boring anyways. Very quiet."

"It's the first date. Maybe she was nervous?"

"Whatever. She's not for me."

"You don't want to give it another shot?"

I thought about it for a second—sitting with Chaya and talking to myself again. The more I thought about it, the more I realized how horrible the date had been. And she made *me* feel bad afterward like I should have sensed the difference in her monotone attitude?

"Nope."

"I'll tell the *shadchan* that you'll try again if she wants. How about that?"

"She won't want to either, believe me."

The next day my mother handed me the phone, "great news," she whispered.

"Chaya really enjoyed herself! She's so thrilled to go out again." The *shadchan* said, "Also, a side point; she did mention that you asked some personal questions she didn't really feel comfortable with so try to be a bit more... understanding next time. Is that alright?"

Slim Chance

I love your blog and I really relate to your stories!!!

I have a story I also wanted to share for all of the frustrated daters out there—and I know it could be hard for you guys but let's be real, the system is way harder on us ladies. I am already married, B"H, but let me tell you, it was hard work getting to this place. Three years of dating literally any guy that would come my way.

The problem with being part of the whole dating game is that the longer you're in it, the worse you feel. It's okay when one guy that you like tells the *shadchanis*, 'she's not my look,' but when it happens quite often and the *shadchanis herself* agrees, giving you outfit ideas and makeup tips, it's downright painful.

So like any girl in the system, I swapped my flats for heels and bought a new primer, foundation, powder and eye shadow palettes from Sephora. I felt fake and I hated it. *This is what Judaism is about?* I thought, *our holy yeshiva boys picking Miss Beauty Queen from the catalog? This is what Hashem intended when he said we each are assigned our* beshert *in* shamayim*?*

But what could we do? We all wanted to get married.

The makeup and clothes may have helped other girls. It didn't help me. I had another problem.

My mother asked the shadchanim straight up why I wasn't being *redt* more *shidduchim*:

"C'mon, she has to lose a few pounds! What can I do? The second I say size eight, they get scared off!"

I have been struggling with my weight since ninth grade, the buttons of my uniform shirt awkwardly pulling against my chest. The few extra pounds used to bother me but I really worked on myself to be okay with my weight. This is the body Hashem gave me after all, and *baruch Hashem* I was healthy.

"Am I fat?" I asked my brother.

He shrugged, "It's a matter of preference. There are for sure guys into bigger women. I have tons of friends who are."

I was twenty-one and he was twenty. I did not need to hear about his generations' preferences. Clearly, all of the twenty-three-year-olds out there were into skinny girls.

That week two girls from my high school class got engaged. They were both size four.

So my mother brought me to a dietician who gave me a complete diet plan and I stuck to my new resolve—I would lose weight.

The diet went like this: three meals a day. Huge meals. Walks three times a week. It was very doable... and it did *not* work. I barely lost a pound the first week.

So, I fashioned my own diet plan.

It was very simple, we learned the formula in biology class. Every day our body burns calories, in order to lose weight, you simply have to take in fewer calories than your body burns. It's like exercising without moving a muscle!

I devised a simple plan. Three meals a day, just like the dietician said—I wanted my diet to be a healthy one—but instead of eating the huge plate of vegetables and proteins, I'd only eat a few bites. It was perfect. I got to taste everything without getting bloated. I could practically feel my stomach burning its fat between meals.

The first week on my diet, I lost five pounds.

My diet also really allowed me to appreciate food and not get caught up in an excessive attitude. Now I'd eat the bites slowly, savoring each flavor.

A few weeks in I got another offer. I hadn't been set up in a while so it was big news. The date was later in the week so I had time to prepare. I cut my five bites down to three and was careful about making sure they weren't full.

I wore a black dress. I couldn't tell if I looked any slimmer but my mother showered me in compliments.

"I've never seen you skinnier!"

The boy was not my type at all, a definite 'no' for me, but amazingly he wanted to go out again! Progress!

From then on it only got easier. If in the beginning, I'd google how many calories a certain food had, a few weeks in, I already knew.

I was lucky my family didn't eat organized suppers all week and when Shabbos came around I'd always busy myself, helping my mother serve.

"When did we raise such a *balabusta*?" my mother beamed to my father.

"She's definitely ready to run a house," my father agreed.

Not yet, I decided as I looked in the mirror. Almost but not yet. I still had a stomach. My shirts still pulled. I could barely fit into a size six and I wanted to be a size four, size two would be even better.

Shabbos was also my time of the week that I could be more lenient with myself, not that I believed what they say about not gaining weight on Shabbos. But it's good to have a little break. I'd let myself a quarter of a *Toffuti* Cutie.

The hardest part, I found, was going out with friends. They always insisted on meeting in a restaurant. Since when did everybody get so obsessed about food?

"You look so great! What's your secret?" they'd gush.

"I am so jealous, how did you lose so much weight?"

I'd just shrug and smile mysteriously.

When we'd order, I'd choose an appetizer from the menu, "I'm not so hungry actually."

"Don't worry," Sara would say, "I'll pay if that's the problem."

How awkward? I'd laugh, "Of course it's not a problem." But there would always be pressure so of course, I'd buy a big salad or a main dish, share a lot of it, eat a bite of it, drink a lot of water and play around with the rest of it on my plate.

It was easier not to go out at all.

Another problem is getting used to the empty feeling in your stomach. It bothered me in the beginning but it's actually quite nice. You really feel the fat slipping off. When it gets really bad you just drink diet juices or soda. It helps.

The diet is also very tiring. Some days even getting out of bed got tiring, let alone going down the stairs and walking to the subway. It's important to have a positive outlook though, or else you'll never get through. You have to know that it's all for the best. The more tired you are means the harder your body is working. It all adds up to more fat being burned!

The diet didn't just make me skinny, my hair started thinning—at first I was concerned, but I wanted to get married soon anyway, this would just make it easier to fit under my wig. My ponytails looked chic and no one noticed, showering me with compliments on my figure.

"I need new dresses," I told my mother when I realized my go-to black date dress hung loose on my body.

That was the glorious day I realized I made it to size four. I'd dropped two sizes! We updated my *shidduch* picture and although in reality I still felt I could lose a few more pounds, I had to admit the photo with my hair up and my tight dress showing off my narrow waist was stunning.

It was around that time that I got set up with handsome, tall, well-to-do Aaron Goldstein—no wonder why.

The first date I wore heels, makeup and a new dress, happy to see it was even a bit baggy at the sides.

The date was perfect. We went out for drinks and I wished all dates would be like this. Just drinks. We laughed, we spoke, we had the same *hashkafa,* and great chemistry. What more does a girl need?

It was clear from date one, yet each date got better and better. I played around with the food on my plate and he barely noticed, too busy looking at my face, worrying if I was cold—I was always cold lately—if my feet hurt from the heels and so on.

By the time we got engaged, I fit into a size two. I wore a long dress with extensions clipped into my hair.

"You look fabulous!"

"You lost so much weight!"

"Wow, you're so skinny."

The compliments at the engagement party were endless.

The revelation in *kallah* classes that I was exempt from so much of those annoying *taharas mishpacha halachos* was relieving—I'd stopped getting my period monthly, B"H.

We got married three months ago, *baruch Hashem.* Aaron is the best husband I could have asked for.

Anyways, I just wanted to share this story to show that even if it seems impossible, unfair, impossibly long, there IS an end.

It's like an uphill battle, and some days you will fail. Some days you will eat the whole Cutie and maybe even two or three! I want you to know that it DOES get better. You WILL lose weight, you WILL look great. You WILL get married!!!

Sometimes the system sucks but you've got to play the system if you want to win... and look at me, I've certainly won.

Black Magic

I was doing everything right. After graduating from high
school, I did the expected year in seminary in Israel. My
parents couldn't afford it, but I threatened them with my
future so they took a loan. *That's how it works*, I patiently
explained to them, *you stay behind, and you lose.* I applied to
college right when I got back, transferring my high school
and seminary credits to nearly half a degree.

Already nineteen years old, my mother wrote me up a
shidduch resume. It wasn't hard. I volunteered throughout

high school with my Down's Syndrome neighbor, my older brother married a rabbi's daughter and younger siblings went to the right schools, I sucked up to my teachers in high school and made a lot of friends. I'm loud and loveable. On the resume, we wrote: friendly and outgoing.

The photo was the hard part. We hired a makeup artist and photographer to help with that. I was only mildly pleased. It's not my fault I have big shoulders and a wide frame, hooded eyes and a prominent nose. I contour daily to narrow it down and splash glitter on my eyelids to make them pop. I'd scroll through Instagram looking at all the dainty girls with envy, trying to imitate their stance that eliminated all trace of excess belly fat, their makeup, the way they tilted their heads just right.

Surprisingly I did get set up. The offers came in a slow trickle, and definitely not the types I was looking for...but at least people had me in mind, right?

I like stylish, I like sexy. I like a man with bigger shoulders than mine, that I can imagine sweeping me off my feet and spinning me in circles. One I could imagine carrying me like a little doll. Why, oh, why do Jewish boys come so short and narrow?

The dates all went similarly painful:

"Nice atmosphere," he'd say.

"Oh yes," I'd answer, wondering what nonexistent atmosphere he'd be referring to and if that was the most interesting thing he could come up with to say. I'd have helped him, I have a knack for storytelling, but I liked to see them try. They'd all try and fail.

"What's the craziest thing you've done?" I'd challenge in an attempt to spice the conversation.

"What do you mean?" At this point, they'd grow nervous, probably wondering if they should tell the truth or if they truly didn't have what to say. I'd hope it was the first.

I'd shrug, "I don't know, the wildest, most insane, out there. The kind of thing you did that even shocked yourself," I asked myself the same question and couldn't come up with one concrete answer, but they didn't have to know.

"I peed on my friend." Disgusting.

"I threw a chair off the roof of my yeshiva." Ridiculous.

"I stole twenty bucks from the *tzedakah* box in my house and used it to buy cigarettes with my uncle's ID." Horrible, horrible, horrible.

I wanted wild, I wanted crazy. I wanted exciting.

But wild, crazy, exciting didn't want me. I stood in front of the mirror squeezing the fat on my arms. They weren't even specifically mushy, just thick and unattractive. A month past

236

Rosh Hashana but it wasn't too late for new resolves. I resolved to shed inches off my frame.

To attain a goal you gotta break it up to pieces, little steps. That's what we learned in seminary. My first step was cardio. I had to switch gyms if I wanted to take this seriously. I went to an all-women's gym. It was stuffy, stale and the treadmills were always full, no matter the hour. It's like none of the women here had a life outside these smelly walls.

The gym down my block was different. It was small and boutique, men lifting weights as they should and a few women running. Always a treadmill available.

For some reason, it felt like a sin walking into the sleek lobby. I knew in my heart of hearts I came here for the treadmills... but would the neighbors know that? Would they think I come to gawk at *goyim* lifting heavy weights with their strong biceps?

So I wore a sweatshirt with a hood hiding my face and went twice a day.

The first time I went I wore a skirt over my leggings. I did it out of modesty but it was possibly the least modest move I could make—everyone stared at me as I ran. With leggings, I blended in. Not as much as I'd have liked with those thin women with abs, but at least I wasn't the sore, fat thumb.

My goal was quashed quite quickly as well. Apparently, it is impossible to actually change the shape of your bone structure. My trainer explained the science of it to me, but he promised I could look cut and tight... and other gym words I'd have to get used to using.

My trainer. I hired him because two hours of running a day became impossible. Because I only lost a pound the first week and had no energy for anything else.

Darius was black, muscular and really smart. He said my cardio plan wasn't healthy, "the point of the gym is to feel better, not worse."

Darius *was* very healthy, he had the perfect gym bod and protein shakes for breakfast and supper.

With his diet and exercise plan, I looked way slimmer by the time I went on my next *shidduch* date.

Moishy worked with stocks and learned in the evenings. He looked tall in the pictures too. He sounded great.

We met and he was short.

"Pleasant atmosphere," he said. Inwardly, I groaned. *Here we go again...*

He told me about a funeral of a distant relative he went to last week, his favorite flavored seltzer, the type of music he listens to (he's not so into Shwekey. Surprising, I know).

I sighed and gave it one last try.

"What's the craziest thing you've done?"

"Hmm, I once left my car double parked for an hour. I thought it would get towed but nothing happened..."

I wanted to cry, to yell, "live a little!" Instead, I told him I was tired and I wanted to go home.

"Hot date last night?" Darius winked as he fetched the weights for our session.

I smiled tightly and ignored him, "how was your evening?"

"Went to the club," he shrugged, "nothing special."

It sounded special to me, and crazy and wild and exciting.

Weeks passed. Dates droned. I copied more makeup tutorials from YouTube and posted the successful selfies on Instagram with my new body that only got better by the day. Look, boys, I wanted to say, look at me now! Don't you want me?

Nope. They still didn't. The trickle of guys I went out with lessened if anything. Lessened because I was being more selective as well. Gone were the days of agreeing to nerdy and slow and thick-rimmed glasses.

Even with my selection, no guy had an impressive enough crazy story.

Craziest thing I did? I bet you're wondering. No one asked me on any date yet but finally, I had an answer. I made out with Darius.

It happened in the storage room. He asked me to help him get some weights out. We both knew what he really wanted, I suspected it already when I saw his likes on the selfies I posted. I was breathless when it was over so I guess it counted as a workout.

I left right after, I didn't want to be too late for my date with Mendy. The *shadchanim* would stop setting me up if they saw I didn't take the dates seriously.

"We're still on for tomorrow?" I asked Darius.

"Whenever you want."

Darius became the highlight of my week. The highlight of my life actually. The rainbow of colors in my drab world of black and white. The rock hard abs in my world of dating flabs. He listened to rap music with the sunroof opened. I joined him because he had tinted windows, between that and my sweatshirt hood, no one would know.

Very soon I found an even better disguise. Gym leggings. No one looked at me twice on the street, their eyes flit right past by, thinking I'm some *goy* with Darius. No neighbor suspected a thing.

"Come out with us tonight," Darius said as I tried to lift my weight in a push-up. I expected it, anticipated it, his invitation. Still, I didn't answer, panting with exertion as my excuse.

"Be ready at ten," he said after the workout. Darius didn't need my answer, he already knew.

My biggest regret was that I spend the whole evening as I waited for him to come, worrying. Worrying and fretting. What should I wear? Who will be there? Will his friends like me? Will they judge me? And of course, the regular doubts: what will Hashem think of me? Will He judge me?

I half expected a bolt of lightning to strike me as I got into Darius's car. He met me at the corner. I told my parents I was going out with a friend and wore a long jacket so they wouldn't see my leggings and a tank top. It wasn't anything new to Darius, he was used to seeing me dressed in shorts and barely dressed at all.

"Hey, Babe," his teeth glowed against his dark chocolate skin and I grinned back.

This was life and I'd make it as crazy, exciting and wild as I could. Live while I'm young, right? Live for all the experiences I'd never have when I'm older, when I'm with some Zevy or Lazer or Mechy and the ungrateful kids that will have me spending my life savings on the school systems that will do them no good.

Hahaha. I laughed out loud and hugged Darius around the neck and said, "You're so dope." And hoped that slang was appropriate.

We danced and drank and the lights hurt my eyes and the music hurt my ears. His friends were so goyish, it was thrilling. They all looked hot and sophisticated and threw back shots unfazed.

I tried to drink like they did and felt woozy but buzzed. We went to another club, more people, more drinks. More sweaty bodies, so unashamed of their sexuality.

In sem we called it *gashmiyus* but no one ever told me *gashmiyus* was so much fun.

And Darius whispered in my ear, "You're so sexy." He said other things too. Things that sounded offensive but that's just slang. We made out in the bathroom. We made out in his car. We almost had sex.

"I'm not ready," I told him. Again and again, until he finally listened.

A month later I was ready. A year later I moved in with him. No more Zevys, Lazers, and Mechys for me. No one but Darius.

My parents didn't respond to the wedding invitation. His friends did. We danced and drank and moved our sophisticated, hot bodies.

It hurt that they didn't come. That we didn't speak anymore, just because of the man I chose to love. Just because I couldn't find anyone else. I couldn't find a nice Jewish boy, I was too ugly for them and they were too boring for me. Hashem knows I tried.

This was life. And as I wrote on Instagram: YOLO.

Darius wrapped his arms around my waist and I knew I was living it right.

Mazal Tov

The date hadn't been great. They had sat for an hour and a half, Chanie doing most of the talking. She wanted Moishy to talk, but every time she asked a question, he'd answer shortly and throw another question her way. It was like he came with a prepared list of questions and was determined to ask every one of them—what her parents do, what her summer plans are, what she liked most about seminary. It felt like a one-sided interview.

"He doesn't have much to say," Chanie told her friend, Mindy. Mindy was a professional dater—by the age of eighteen she'd been to every *shadchan* in town. Chanie was new in the *parsha* and after every date she'd call on Mindy for advice.

"Maybe he was nervous, or shy. It could be his first time going out. You never know," Mindy said, "But besides for that, did everything else go well?"

"Besides for what, his *personality*?" Chanie asked incredulously, "Yeah, on paper he's great—he's in a good yeshiva, I think he's smart, his family sounds cute... we just didn't have such a good time."

"Well, I usually give the guy at least two dates before I say no. Unless it's *really* horrible."

"*Uch*, but personality, it's huge! I don't even want someone shy and nervous. I want someone confident and fun!"

"Whatever," Mindy shrugged, "do what you want."

Chani agreed to give Moishy another shot.

It was Moishy's first ever date and he was nervous as heck. He asked everyone he knew for advice—the *shadchan*, his cousins, his parents, his friends.

"You have to figure out the basics. Ask about her family. "

"Let her talk. She'll feel special."

"Figure out how she views life. Maybe ask how her year in seminary was?"

"Pay attention to everything she says."

They sat in a café and the time just flew by. Before he knew it, his silent alarm buzzed in his pocket signalling an hour and a half, the ideal first date time he was told.

Chanie always had what to say, on every topic. He could listen to her all day. That way he wouldn't have to speak himself and risk messing up. All he had to do was rub his sweaty palms on his pants under the table, nod and prompt her as soon as she finished answering. This dating thing was a breeze.

"She wants to go out again? Yes!" he pumped his fist, surprised himself at how excited he was. He had to calm down. An hour and a half with one girl, he shouldn't be so sure of this... Moishy grinned despite himself.

"You have to give me a real answer this time," Chanie said.

"I have been giving you real answers," Moishy said, confused.

"*No.* You are answering everything with one sentence answers. You can't just tell me Shavuos was good. You have to tell me *how* and *why*. Who did you learn with? Did you stay up all night? I want details!"

Chanie took a deep breath and realized that perhaps she overreacted. It was only halfway into the second date. She decided not to regret telling him off. It wasn't fair to make her do all the talking.

Moishy was stumped. *Let her talk. She'll feel special.* Who gave him that advice? His seventeen-year-old cousin Shaya? What did that kid know?

"Right, of course, I just didn't think—" he started from the beginning, "Shavuos was great. There's such special energy in the Beis Medrash. I napped the whole day before so I'd have energy but I still managed to pass out for an hour or two around four a.m...." he laughed and shrugged, "was that better?"

Chanie smiled, "much better. Now it's my turn to ask *you* questions."

It was like a flip switched, Chanie asked, Moishy answered, Chanie commented, Moishy commented back. Conversation flowed.

When Mindy called for updates the next day, Chanie couldn't hold back her smile, "it went well. Really well."

"Where do you see yourself in ten years?" Moishy asked after telling Chanie about his professional goals. His father owned real estate and needed a manager. Moishy was good at dealing with people, except for dealing with girls on first dates apparently.

"Hmm. Ten years is a long time. *Im'yirzeh Hashem*, I'd want a few kids and a nice home."

"Such a short answer," Moishy teased.

Chanie laughed, "You're right. I just don't want to make any *ayin haras*."

"*Bli ayin hara*, you deserve the best."

Moishy and Chanie smiled at each other and couldn't stop. *She deserved Moishy*, she thought, *he was definitely the best*.

By date one, Moishy knew. By date five, he *really* knew. By date ten, he told her.

"I feel like this is it, Chanie. I feel like you're the one."

Chanie just nodded because she knew whatever it was that Moishy was feeling. There were no words that could describe it, just the mutual feeling that everything was right.

"It's too soon," Chanie's mother said, "you have to go out longer, you have to see."

But Chanie already knew.

A lot happened in the next few days. They met with the parents for a *l'chaim*. It was very formal and everybody was stiff and polite, Moishy's father cracked jokes. Chanie's mother hated jokes. Moishy's mother had a migraine and had to excuse herself to the car. Chanie's father was very excited, very talkative and very awkward.

None of that mattered. Chanie and Moishy glowed the whole time.

By their engagement party, Chanie hugged Mindy tight and gave her the biggest *bracha* to find her *beshert* soon.

"Really," Chanie whispered, "thank you so much."

Moishy looked so nice in his brand new suit and tie. Chanie looked stunning in her baby pink gown.

The wedding was two months away and Moishy and Chanie counted every minute, wishing they'd set the date earlier.

They couldn't wait to start a life together.

"After a day of learning, I'll come home to my beautiful wife."

"I'll make us a gourmet supper."

"And afterwards... do you like chess?"

"You could teach me."

They *mamish* couldn't wait.

Glossary

The following glossary provides a partial explanation of some of the Hebrew, Yiddish, and Aramaic words and phrases used in this book. The spelling and explanations reflect the way the specific word is used herein. Often, there are alternate spellings and meanings for the words.

Abba: father

Avos: forefathers

Ayin hara: the evil eye

Balabusta: a good homemaker

Baruch Hashem (abbreviated B"H): Thank G-d

Beshert: soulmate

Bench: blessing after meals

Binah: understanding

Bochur: a young man

Bracha/brachos: blessing/s

Bubbeh maises: grandmother's tales

Chas v'shalom: G-d forbid

Chavrusa/chavruta: a Torah study partner

Chazer: pig

Chuppah: the wedding canopy

Chatan/chosson: groom

Cholav stam: milk not derived under the supervision of an observant Jew

Daven: pray

Dor Yesharim: genetic screening through this nonprofit organization, to prevent fatal and debilitating recessive genetic disorders in the Jewish community

Dvar Torah: words of Torah

Eretz Yisroel: Israel

Frum: religious

Gaayvadik: haughty

Gashmiyus: physical pleasures

Goyish: non-Jewish

Hakaras hatov: appreciation

Halacha: Jewish law

Halachic prenup: A prenuptial agreement to prevent woman from becoming an 'agunah,' tied to the marriage against her will

Hashem: G-d

Hashgacha pratis: Divine guidance

Hashkafa: outlook on levels of observance

Heter: rabbinic allowance

Hechsher: Kosher certification

Im yirtze Hashem (abbreviated I"H) : if G-d wills it

Ima: mother

'In the parsha' (expression): somebody looking to get married

Kallah: bride

Kallah moyd: marriageable girl

Kavanah: sincere intention

Keser Torah: crown for decoration of Torah

Kiddush: sanctification of the Sabbath and festivals usually recited over a cup of wine or grape juice

Masechta: Talmudic tractate

Makolet: convenience store

Mazal tov: phrase to express congratulations

Mehadrin: the most stringent level of kosher supervision

Middah/middos: virtue/s

Mincha: afternoon prayer

Minhag/im: custom/s

Min haShamayim/miShamayim: from G-d

Mitzvah/mitzvos: commandment/s, popularly understood as a good deed

Motzei Shabbos: Saturday evening

Neshama: soul

Nisayon: test or trial

'Off the derech' (expression): left the Orthodox community

Oleh chadash: new immigrant to Israel

Oneg Shabbos: celebratory gathering held on Shabbos

Parsha: weekly Torah portion

Parve: neither milk nor meat

Perek: chapter

Rav: a rabbi

Rebbe: teacher or mentor

Redt: offered a potential match

Refuah shelaima: a blessing for complete recovery

Seder: time devoted to learning during the day

Sefer: holy book

Sem: abbreviated seminary

Sheva brachos: the week of celebration after the wedding

Sfira/Sfirat ha'Omer: The counting of the Omer. A period of time between Pesach and Shavuot

Shachris: morning prayer

Shadchan/shadchanit: matchmaker

Shamayim: the heavens

Shechita: method of Kosher slaughter

Shayach: relevant

Sheitel: wig

Shidduch/shidduchim: marriage proposals

Shidduch Crisis: The Shidduch crisis is a commonly observed and discussed phenomenon in the Orthodox Jewish community whereby eligible single persons, especially women, have difficulty finding a suitable spouse

Shiur: lesson

Shmone Esrei: the silent, standing prayer

Shomer (negiah): the halachic prohibition on touching members of the opposite sex

Shul: a synagogue

Tachlis: the real deal

Taharas mishpacha: laws of family purity in accordance with Jewish law

Tatty: daddy

Taiva: desire

Teshuva: repentance

Tznius: modesty

Yeshiva: an academy of Torah study

Yerushalayim: Jerusalem

Yetzer Hara: evil inclination

Yichud room: secluded room for bride and groom after marriage

Yiddeshe neshama: Jewish soul

Yontif: holiday

Acknowledgments

Writing this book was a big project and like all big projects, it couldn't have been done alone. First, I have to thank Hashem for pouring words into my brain when I needed them, and when I didn't need them—three in the morning, about to fall asleep, when an idea pops into my head.

And then of course, my family, whose attention I have been very demanding of lately. I'd like to name you all specifically but it will take up too much space. You know who you are!

Specifically, I'd like to thank Tzippy, my first reader, brainstorm buddy and biggest fan, you were with me from start to end, holding my hand and pushing me when needed. And Eli, so much of this was your vision. I hope it lives up to our expectations.

Thank you Saba, Ima and Abba, you are always so supportive of me, pushing me to follow my dreams even if they aren't so conventional.

To my early readers, especially Penina, who read these stories, often in first drafts on printed papers or on your tiny cell phone screens, your feedback made these stories better.

This was a whole lot of work and a whole lot of fun. Thank you to everyone who followed and supported my journey, from day one until the end.

About the Author

Penina Shtauber, an artist and travel enthusiast, enjoys writing, barbeques, and yoga. She grew up in New York and lives in Israel.

CPSIA information can be obtained
at www.ICGtesting.com
Printed in the USA
BVHW040307201221
624348BV00007B/154

9 789659 275700